FREE GIFTS FROM
THE ARMADA COLLECTORS' CLUB

Look out for these tokens in your favourite Armada series! All you need to do to receive a special FREE GIFT is collect 6 tokens in the same series and send them off to the address below with a postcard marked with your name and address including postcode. Start collecting today!

Send your tokens to:

Armada Collectors' Club
HarperCollins Children's Books,
77 - 85 Fulham Palace Road,
London, W6 8JB

Or if you live in New Zealand to:

Armada Collectors' Club
HarperCollins Publishers Ltd.
31 View Road, Glenfield,
PO Box 1, Auckland

THIS OFFER APPLIES TO RESIDENTS OF THE U.K., EIRE AND NEW ZEALAND ONLY.

1 TOKEN

CS

The Chalet School series by Elinor M. Brent-Dyer

Excitements at the Chalet School

Elinor M. Brent-Dyer

Armada
An Imprint of HarperCollins*Publishers*

To Rose, with much love from Elinor

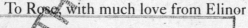

First published in 1957 by Chambers Ltd
First published in paperback in 1981 by
William Colllins Sons & Co. Ltd.
This impression 1993

Armada is an imprint of HarperCollins Children's Books,
a division of HarperCollins Publishers Ltd,
77–85 Fulham Palace Road, Hammersmith,
London W6 8JB

Copyright © Elinor M. Brent-Dyer 1957

Printed and bound in Great Britain by
HarperCollins Book Manufacturing Ltd, Glasgow.

CONTENTS

CHAPTER ONE

THE PREFECTS AND INTER V

"You can say what you like! I still maintain and always shall, that of all the forms in this school, Inter V has the biggest supply of utter *brats*!" Blossom Willoughby paused a moment for breath, but before anyone else could butt in, she was off again. "Just count them over! Heather Clayton—Margot Maynard—Emerence Hope—Francie Wilford—Betty Landon—"

"All that's wrong with Betty," at this point, Mary-Lou, the library prefect, interrupted what looked like being a list of almost all Inter V, "is that she and tact aren't even on speaking terms. There's no real harm in the kid," she went on, sublimely ignoring the fact that the said "kid" was barely fifteen months younger than herself. "She *means* quite well. Her trouble is that if she *can* talk of rope in a house where there's been a hanging, she does it, *con amore*!"

"You've said it!" This was Lesley Bethune, the second hobbies prefect. She grinned at Mary-Lou and then turned to the irate Blossom. "What's all this in aid of, Blossom, my pet? Who's been doing what to our poppet?"

Blossom, head of the games at the Chalet School, had had time to cool down. Now she sat down on the chair her chum, Sybil Russell, had pulled from the table and patted invitingly, made a face at Lesley and then mopped her brow with her handkerchief.

"I know we're warm in here," Elinor Pennell, the Head Girl, remarked, "but I shouldn't have thought it was as torrid as all that! Come off it, Blossom! What's been happening and why is Inter V the target for your scorn?"

Blossom put away her handkerchief and sat up. "Well, you all know what the weather's been like almost ever since we came back this term?"

7

"We do—we do!" It came as a chorus from the entire body of prefects.

"We've had literally *no* outdoor exercise since Friday—and this is Tuesday! It's meant arranging anything we can for everyone to keep them going and that's none too easy."

"Oh, do go on!" Lala Winterton, who was responsible for stationery, exclaimed impatiently. "Get on with what's happened this afternoon and hurry up about it! The bell will be ringing for Kaffee und Kuchen any time now and then we'll have to go."

"Well, this morning Burnie sent for me and said it was games period for Inter V this afternoon and as she'd offered to take the Thirds for their dictation and repetition she couldn't do it. So she asked me to take it on. Said I might ask anyone I liked to help me. The only thing was that I was to exercise the little pets thoroughly and shake the fidgets out of them. Of course I said, 'Can do'—or words to that effect. I asked round and found that Vi Lucy and Hilda Jukes were free as neither of them takes science, so I collected them and we made up a nice programme for them—something calculated to make the entire lot be thankful to sit quiet and get on with their prep without a fuss this evening."

"What did you do?" Sybil asked curiously.

"I proposed bean bags to start them off. Then I thought we'd have a round of country dancing with things like *Goddesses* and *Old Mole* and *Picking up Sticks*—the sort of things that take the vim out of you quite a little. Then I was going to give them frog racing because you can do that by heats which gives people a chance to rest a few minutes in between." Blossom paused and looked at them all.

"If you got all that in," Lala said, "I should think the only thing they'd be fit for would be *bed*! Cruelty to dumb animals, I call it!"

"Well," Blossom went on, "we got it all worked out and Vi offered to play for the dancing. She's awfully good, you know. Then Hilda suggested that it would be a good idea to *begin* with the dancing and let them have bean bags as

8

a rest between that and frog racing, so that's what we fixed on."

"Well?" Elinor asked as the narrator paused a moment. "Go on!"

"They were all waiting for us, and Hilda and I got them into sets and we gave them a good twenty minutes of it. By the time we finished up—we added a *Sellenger's Round* for good measure—they were all boiling hot and quite ready to sit quietly for a minute or two. And that, my loves, was where the fun started."

"How?" Mary-Lou asked concisely.

"I said we'd have bean bags and they could rest while I got the bags out. Hilda came to help me and I heard two distinct gasps as I went to the cupboard. I didn't think anything of it at the time—just thought someone was being ostentatious. Anyhow, when I lifted the first bags, I nearly dropped 'em!"

"*What*? But what on earth *for*?" demanded Hilary Bennet, who was second library prefect and who had been listening to this enthralling yarn without saying anything.

"Because they were so heavy." The dents in Blossom's cheeks suddenly deepened as she added. "And I only wonder I didn't yell!"

"But—*why*?" Elinor asked, sitting very erect.

"Because, my sweetie-pie, those little wretches had been at the bags earlier on and emptied the beans out of them and filled them chock-a-block with emery-powder! I should say," Blossom added dreamily, "that each of those bags weighed at least a pound."

Mary-Lou most reprehensibly giggled. "Gosh! I'd have liked to see them trying to heave *that* lot around!"

"But where on earth did they get so much?" Sybil asked, amazement in her voice.

"Not knowing, can't say. But I did institute immediate inquiries and Emerence and Margot owned up that *they* had done it—not knowing that they'd be using the things themselves. They meant it for Va who seem to have got their collective goat somehow. They didn't go into details and I felt it was wiser to let well alone."

9

"Oh, *I* can tell you about that!" Nan Herbert, editor of *The Chaletian*, interposed. "I landed into the middle of it. It was really Virginia Adams who began it all. You know what a bossy creature she is? Well, some of Inter V were kicking up a row in their form room last night after prep. We were just finishing with the Head's lecture on Chaucer, but I had to go to seek a hanky. I heard the row and went to quell it. When I got there, I found Virginia, finding there was no prefect on duty, had taken it on herself to go and shut them up."

"She *would*!" Sybil butted in. She had long had a feud with the said Virginia and so far neither had showed the slightest sign of letting it drop.

"Yes; it's exactly like her," assented Nan who was not too fond of Virginia herself. "Anyhow, when I got there, Virginia was shouting at them to be quiet and stop making all that din. Heather Clayton cheeked her—told her *she* wasn't a prefect and had no right to come and order them about. That was where *I* arrived and the little wretches saw me and became dead silent which was as pointed a snub as you could imagine. Virginia hadn't the sense to let it drop. She turned on me and demanded that I report them for noisiness and impudence. I ticked them off all right and told Heather to take an order mark and apologise to Virginia for rudeness. And," Nan went on, indignation in her voice, "the young demon had the sauce to say, 'Oh, I'm sorry, Nan. I didn't know Virginia had become a sub-prefect. I apologise, Virginia. It was a mistake on my part.' I could have wrung her neck with pleasure!"

The prefects lay back in their chairs and screamed with laughter. No one was fond of Virginia who nursed two grievances—first, that she had not been promoted to VIb at the beginning of the year and therefore—second—that she was not even a sub-prefect, though she was several months older than a good many girls who were prefects. Heather's repartee struck them as definitely funny.

"What happened then?" Hilary asked when she had recovered.

"I chucked the lot of them out. I didn't quite know

what to say to Heather, so I thought it best to say nothing. What would *you* have done?"

"The same, probably. Virginia would have been even madder if you'd pointed out that she *wasn't* a sub. I hope to goodness it ended there?" Elinor looked rather anxious.

"Well, it didn't. She went and reported them to Miss Ferrars—over my head, too! Ferry asked if *no* prefect had been there and when she heard I had been and what I'd done, wanted to know what else Virginia wanted. That, I believe, ended it. Ferry's all there, isn't she?"

Rightly regarding this as a rhetorical question, Elinor merely turned to Blossom and demanded to be told what she had done about the bean bags.

"I told Inter V exactly what I thought of their cheek in messing about with gym apparatus at all. My thoughts," Blossom added with entire satisfaction, "weren't at all flattering! Then I told them they could use their free time after prep and make those bean bags right again. Then, as bean bags was off—I wasn't risking anyone being knocked out by getting a pound or so of emery-powder on the head!—I put them on to frog racing. That was all right so long as they were doing the heats. There were eighteen of them present—the great Yseult was having her music lesson by that time, thank goodness!—so I divided them into threes and took the winner of each three to hop in the final. And what did they do? They solemnly hopped to meet each other and the end was a lovely mix-up on the floor with Jo Scott at the bottom of the heap. You should just have seen her when Vi and Hilda and I had got the other five hauled off her! She'd landed on her face and—well, I know the gym is properly swept out every day, but it must accumulate a terrific amount of dust in the course of the day. Anyhow, Jo was simply filthy—dust from head to foot! And, of course, Matey *had* to be passing at that moment and came in to see what all the noise was about. She saw Jo in the full beauty of it all and I thought she was going to have a fit!"

"Was she very awful?" Hilary asked sympathetically.

"Not before the kids. She whisked Jo off at top speed to

11

change and bath and wash her hair which looked *grey* with dust. But she sent for me when the bell went and I heard *all* about it! What she had to say about the keeping of the younger girls in order being our business was nobody's affair!"

Sybil Russell laughed. "Poor old Blossom! You *have* had a time of it!"

"You know," Hilary Bennet mused, "I'm beginning to think that the Heads have made a mistake for once. That form should never have been included among the seniors. I was helping Miss Dene to work out average ages at the end of last term and do you know what the average is for Inter V? Just exactly fifteen!"

"They wouldn't be as low as that if they didn't have the Maynard trio there," Lesley Malcolm pointed out. "Those three are only thirteen and that pulls down the age average a lot. I should have said that apart from them it was a lot more likely to be fifteen-six or so."

"Yes; but aren't those three balanced by people like Yseult Pertwee and Joan Baker—oh, and Caroline Sanders?" Elinor asked. "Joan and Caroline are both well over sixteen and that awful Pertwee girl must be nearly seventeen. So you get a difference that way, too. I should say they cancelled each other out."

"Is Yseult Pertwee nearly seventeen?" Mary-Lou asked in startled tones. "What on earth is she doing in a form like Inter V at that rate? She ought to be in Va at lowest. When's she seventeen? Do you know, Hilary?"

Hilary nodded. "I got a shock myself when I was working it out. She's seventeen at the end of March— older than you and I, my dear."

"*And*, from all I can hear, has a sticky time keeping her end up there," put in Lala. "And if Inter V were a Middle School form, Hilary, just you remember that girl would be in Vb and she'd be even more bother there than she is in Inter. Why on earth her mother wanted to unload the creature on us is more than I can guess. She's the world's worst creep and as ignorant as they come."

"Slang—slang!" said Blossom reprovingly; and the rebuke, coming from *that* source, was so outrageous that Lala was breathless and Hilary took up the tale again.

"Well, I don't know what the rest of you think, but it strikes me that it behoves us to sit up and take a little more notice of Inter V than we've done, so far. It's quite bad enough having imps in the Fourths and Thirds without having to tackle the same among the Fifths."

Lesley Bethune spoke. "The trouble is," she said, "that actually, they're neither fish, flesh, fowl, nor good red herring—by which I mean they're hardly seniors and yet they're a little beyond middles—most of them, anyway—and it's a muddling position to be in. They don't know what to make of themselves and if we don't look out, we're not going to know what to make of them, either."

Her clan listened to her with respect. Lesley was a silent creature for the most part, but she was a thinker and when she did talk, her crowd had got into the habit of listening to her. Mary-Lou went as deeply as she—in some ways deeper; but she was a chatterer, too, though they were all ready to listen to *her*. On this occasion, Elinor turned to the first library prefect to ask, "What do you think, Mary-Lou? Is that what's likely to be the trouble?"

Mary-Lou had been regarding Lesley thoughtfully. "Yes," she said, in reply to Elinor's query. "I think Lesley's got at a lot of the truth. But I also think we'll have to go further than that."

"In what way?" It was Madge who asked this.

"Well, some of them have come on a good deal since the beginning of last term and *are* beginning to take a more—more—*adult* stand. It's a terribly mixed form. I don't believe," she added with a sudden rush of inspiration, "that we can possibly lump them all together and treat them all the same way. You get girls like Jo Scott and Rosamund Lilley who look at things from—well, from *our* point of view, more or less. And then you get people like Margot Maynard and Heather Clayton who are still middles in their outlook and likely to remain so for a while yet. If you ask me, it's a difficult form and we'll have to move carefully where they're concerned—especially," she added with a sudden grin, "when you remember that they've also got Yseult Pertwee who fancies herself grown-up and who can behave in a thoroughly kiddish way."

The young faces round the table in the prefects' room were very grave as they listened to their other oracle. Sybil looked at Lesley.

"Do you agree, Lesley?" she asked.

Lesley nodded. "Every time! If you notice, you'll see that they aren't a united form. They're broken up into little cliques all the way through. They've had a whole term to grow together, but I haven't seen any sign of its happening so far. Oh, I know it's too early in the term to say definitely yet. We haven't been back a full week. But that's how it struck me at the end of last term and I haven't seen anything to show that they're any different this."

Blossom nodded. "I see what you mean. But, I say! That's going to make things jolly difficult all round isn't it? I mean it's going to mean that we'll have to think a lot when we're dealing with them."

"That won't hurt you!" Elinor retorted. "Do you all the good in the world! The trouble with you is that except for games, you never bother to think enough." She looked round the table. "Has it ever struck you what a hard row it makes for Miss Ferrars to hoe? It didn't me until Lesley and Mary-Lou spoke just now."

"Don't you worry about Miss Ferrars," Blossom said. "She's got everything it takes and then some!"

"And who's talking slang now, I'd like to know?" Lala demanded.

"Me! And while I think of it do you all realise that ever since this matter started we've all been breaking rules as hard as ever we could go? This is Tuesday, isn't it?— French day! How much French has a single one of us spoken?"

"Satan rebuking Satan!" Mary-Lou said with a grin. She added in French, "But you're quite right, Blossom. We can hardly go ticking people off and fining them for

14

forgetting when we do it *ad lib* ourselves. We'd better be careful."

"It's Blossom's fault," Hilary said, her blue eyes dancing at Blossom's indignant face. "Oh, yes, it is, my dear! If you hadn't come bursting in here as if wolves were after you, we should have remembered before this."

Blossom's eyes flashed and she looked furious for a moment. Then she suddenly dissolved into giggles. "I'll take the blame this time. And there goes the bell for Kaffee und Kuchen. We'd better go downstairs to see that the little dears make nice neat lines and march quietly into the Speisesaal. Come along, folks! Do your duty as good little prefects! And all of you! Keep a firm eye on Inter V. It strikes me they're going to need it this term!"

CHAPTER TWO

INTER V HOLD A MEETING

INTER V had decided to hold a meeting. That is to say about half of them had. The rest had flatly refused to have anything to do with it. They might be angry at the way Virginia Adams, who wasn't even a sub-prefect, had tried to interfere with them the previous evening, but they couldn't see that holding an indignation meeting would make any difference. Anyhow, as Alicia Leonard had pointed out, she got nothing by it. Miss Ferrars had simply asked questions until she discovered the entire unadorned story and then told Virginia that she couldn't see what more she wanted.

Len Maynard, when tackled, dismissed the whole thing as "tripe of the tripiest kind" and Con, who generally followed her lead, had added simply, "There'll only be another row and term's just begun. How many *do* you want in the term, Francie?"

Francie Wilford was the leader of the malcontents. Her followers included the naughtiest girls in the form— Heather Clayton, Charmian Spence, new the previous term and an imp of the first order, Emerence Hope, Margot Maynard—a pair of promising firebrands, though recent events had caused them to sober down a little— and Betty Landon who was more thoughtless than sinful and given to joining in anything that could be described as "a rag".

These six had drifted naturally together and formed a strong clique in the form. Margot and Emerence contrived to keep out the worst mischief—both had suffered too much during the past year or so from falling into it to wish to do anything else—but the remaining four were demons of the first order.

The other two of Maynard triplets kept well out of it. Len had a well-developed sense of responsibility as became the eldest—by half-an-hour!—of nine; and Con, who had inherited to the full their mother's gift of writing, was generally too busy with her imaginary people to worry much about outside affairs.

With these two were joined Jo Scott, Rosamund Lilley and two newcomers, Eve Hurrell and Pamela Jackson. This six represented most of the common sense of Inter V. Of the rest, Joan Baker, having made an appallingly bad beginning two terms previously, had turned right round and was working tooth and nail to make up huge gaps in her education and, in any case, was a young lady of some sophistication who dubbed efforts like the present one "kiddish" in the extreme. Yseult Pertwee at nearly seventeen was neither asked nor expected to join in and would have refused, since her present attitude was to keep aloof from girls mainly two years younger than herself because she felt their antics very much beneath her dignity. The rest were too full of their own ploys to be forever in rebellion, besides being law-abiding on the whole.

On this occasion, however, the majority of Inter V felt that they had a legitimate grievance. It was no part of the duties of Va girls to come and interfere in their doings. Granted they had been making rather more noise than was either necessary or desirable; it was no business of Virginia Adams's and she had no right to come and interfere. Therefore, quite a number of the saner members of the form joined up with the firebrands and came to the meeting Francie had called that afternoon during the brief interval between lessons and Kaffee und Kuchen, their afternoon meal.

Since the snow was still falling heavily, it must be held indoors and it had taxed all their ingenuity to think of somewhere they could be reasonably sure of not being interrupted. Francie had finally hit on the form's splashery, not the most ideal of places, but at least somewhere where they might hope to be free from unwelcome visitors at that hour when most of the school would be upstairs in the dormitories, changing for the evening.

"But what about us changing?" Margot Maynard had asked when Francie first mooted the question of holding an indignation meeting.

"We'll just have to keep an eye on the time and leave —say, ten minutes to change. You can do it in that, surely?"

"O.K.; I'll be along," Margot said easily. "I must say I think it's a bit *much* when girls from Va come barging in on us and try to boss us all over the shop!"

The rebels assembled in the splashery. A more inconvenient place for a form meeting could hardly have been imagined. It was a long, narrow slip of a room with pegs round three walls and a big stand with other pegs running down the centre. At one end were the lockers where they kept their shoes and slippers and which they were supposed to use for no other purpose. Opposite was the wide window with three toilet basins with hot and cold water beneath. Francie, as chairman, perched herself on the broad windowsill, her long legs dangling over the centre basin in imminent peril of turning on one or other of the taps whenever she moved suddenly. The remainder, some ten or twelve girls, leaned against the walls and all eyes turned to the chairman who was finding her seat more impressive than comfortable.

"We'll have to talk very quietly," she began. "If you have anything to say, put up your hand and I'll call on you

17

in turn. I'll speak first as I called the meeting. Now! You all know what that ass Virginia Adams did yesterday. She walked in on us and tried to order us about and she isn't even a *sub*-prefect! And when Nan who, I *will* say, had the right to do it, ticked us off and ladled out an order mark to Heather and then told us to clear out and do it quietly, wanted to end there, what did Virginia do?" In spite of her own preliminary warning, her voice shrilled and rose with her indignation. "She had the cheek to say we ought to be reported! I ask you!"

Francie had begun in French, but as her feelings got the better of her, she forgot and dropped into English. It was at this point that Margot Maynard's hand shot up. Francie looked at her severely.

"You can't speak yet," she said. "I'm not nearly finished. You wait till then."

"No, but for goodness' sake, stick to French!" Margot implored, forgetting to speak it herself in her agitation. "We don't want to be fined the earth and have nothing but church collections on Saturday—at least *I* don't!"

"And what are *you* talking?" the chairman asked with point. Then, as Margot went red, she continued in French which was fluent enough when she chose, though the less said about the accent the better!

"And when Nan refused to do anything more, what did that—that *cat* do? She went and reported us herself over Nan's head—and Nan's a *prefect*!"

"How do you know that?" someone asked with great interest.

"I heard her doing it after Kaffee und Kuchen. I was going upstairs to fetch a hanky and she'd caught Ferry and was telling her all about it like mad."

"But Ferry hasn't said anything to us about it," someone else objected.

"Did you expect her to?" Francie demanded. "Ferry's fair whatever else she is. Nan had ticked us off and handed Heather her order mark *and* made her apologise—though I must say, Heather, your apology was the limit!"

18

Heather chuckled. "I did rather get home at her, didn't I? Well, what is all this in aid of. Ferry hasn't taken any notice or we'd have heard about it before now."

"No one ever thought she would. I *said* Ferry was fair! Besides it's the *principle* of the thing. I mean, we have the staff *and* the prees to jump on us if they think it necessary. If we're going to let Va do it as well, life won't be worth living!"

"It's only Virginia so far," Alicia Leonard pointed out. "Most of the others wouldn't be likely to— not unless we *shoved* ourselves on their notice."

"You let it go on and sooner or later it'll be the whole lot!" Francie retorted—most unfairly, since the majority of Va considered that it would be time enough for them to worry about prefect duties when they were full-blown prefects and preferred a quiet life to interfering with those demons in Inter V.

Heather suddenly giggled again. "I say! *Did* you notice Virginia's face when I told her I didn't know she'd been appointed a sub-pree? I nearly collapsed!"

The meeting showed signs of incipient hysteria at this joyful memory and Francie hushed them in a vigorous undertone. "Shut up, idiots—I mean, taisez-vous donc, vous sottes! Si personne nous écoute, elle viendra. Voulez-vous des order-marks?"

No one did and they pulled themselves together at the reminder. Francie thereupon concluded her speech. "Well, that is all, I think—except that, as I said, if we don't want the whole of Va interfering with us, we must stop it at once."

"But *how*?" Betty Landon asked, looking puzzled.

Before anyone could reply, there came the sound of flying footsteps and the next moment, Len Maynard had irrupted into their midst. "Clear out, all of you, unless you want to get into a row!" she exclaimed in good English. Her next sentences were in French, however. "Matey's coming to do a locker-raid—I heard her telling Elinor so. You must fly at once or you'll be caught and she'll want to know what you're all doing here when you're

19

supposed to be in your cubicles, changing for the evening."

If it had been only the Head Girl herself, they might have braved it out. But the girl had yet to be born who would have outfaced Matron when she was on the war-path—and a locker-raid indicated that she was very much so. They began to scramble to the door, their grievances forgotten before present danger. Luckily Francie, who was not quite devoid of common sense, stopped the first wild flight.

"Stop it, idiots! You can't all scram like that at once! If anyone see you there'll be trouble. Go by two or threes and don't be such asses!" she said.

She tempted providence heavily by making these re-marks in English but, although none of them ever knew this, the Head had sent for Matron just before she set off and they got away with it for once. They took Francie's advice in fear and trembling, but they took it. By twos and threes they left the place to walk demurely to the foot of the stairs. But then they flung all caution to the winds and went scuttering up them like a bunch of startled rabbits. Luckily for them, most people had finished changing and gone down to the common rooms to await the welcome bell for Kaffee und Kuchen which, in the Swiss Oberland, took the place of tea at this hour. The only person to be caught was the unlucky Francie herself. Racing down the corridor to reach Pansy dormitory, she ran plump into the arms of Mary-Lou, nearly overturning that young woman and sliding over the polished boards herself in a way that nearly sent her headlong to the door-way. Mary-Lou caught her in time and steadied her.

"Well, and why are you so late coming up to change?" she demanded in her prettily-accented French.

"I—was busy," Francie gasped. She had twisted herself slightly and Mary-Lou's arrival on the scene when, by all rights, she should have been in the prefects' room, was an additional shock. "I'll be quick, Mary-Lou."

"Your accent," Mary-Lou pronounced dispassionately, "is horrible. All right. There isn't time now to correct you, but you can come to me before prep and I'll show you how to say that correctly. Can you manage in time by yourself?"

"Yes, thank you," Francie said. "At least, oui, merci bien."

"*That's* better!" Mary-Lou said austerely. "You try hard, Francie and you'll soon have a decent accent. You said that very well." Then she turned on her heel and went striding off towards the main staircase as was her right and privilege as a prefect.

Francie stood for a moment, staring after her. "Well, Mary-Lou's all right, anyhow!" she muttered to herself as she cast off tunic and blouse and wriggled into her velveteen with frantic haste. "There's not time to wash. I'll just sponge my face over and tidy my hair and that'll have to do."

She made it do and, as a result, was grabbed by Blossom Willoughby who desired to know why she had come to table with such filthy hands.

"You might be a junior!" the disgusted games prefect said. "Look at your *nails*! 'Black' doesn't begin to describe them! Off you go to the splashery and do something about them. And never come to table like that again unless you want an order mark!"

Francie went because there was nothing else to do. But the look she cast after Blossom's retreating back was so malevolent that Emerence Hope, turning in time to get the full beauty of it, gave a stifled exclamation.

But Blossom's rather tactless remarks had settled things for Francie. You had to put up with such things from the prefects. After all, that was what they were there *for*. But Va weren't going to do it or she would know the reason why!

CHAPTER THREE

WINTER-SPORTING

AFTER Kaffee und Kuchen, Mary-Lou caught Francie, who
had been fully prepared to forget her command, led her
off to a quiet spot, and proceeded to make her repeat
"Je m'occupais des affaires. Je me dépêcherai" until it
came with a distinctly more French accent than the original
statement had done. When they had arrived at this point,
the prefect grinned.

"*That's* more like it! Now try to remember for the
future. After all, one reason why we're here is so that we
learn to speak languages properly. And it isn't as if you
were stupid you know. Far from it! You've all the brains
anyone could ask if you'd only use them. All right; you
may go now."

With this, she released Francie and that young woman
had just time to tear to the form room and get out her
books before the bell rang for prep. That meant that there
was no chance just then of renewing the meeting which
Len had interrupted—and just as well, perhaps.

Francie had fully intended to summon her followers
after Abendessen and prayers, but during the meal, Miss
Annersley announced that they were to have folk dancing
in Hall after prayers and it would go on all the evening.
They had had very little real exercise since the Friday and
a good many of them were becoming touchy and irritable.
She had decided that an hour and a half of all the more
strenuous folk dances would help to shake the fidgets out
of them and clear the atmosphere.

Miss Burnett, the games mistress had been called on to
produce a programme which would accomplish this, and
as she acted as caller, she kept them hard at it until, when
the prefects finally departed bedwards, every girl in the
school was so tired that she was thankful to lie down and
go to sleep.

To continue the treatment, the snow stopped before

midnight. A bitter wind from the polar regions brought severe frost with it and when, after Frühstück as they called it in the Oberland, the light had strengthened sufficiently for them to see out of the windows, it was to behold a white and icy world. The sun rose, pale and glittering and under his rays, the outside landscape sparkled everywhere.

"Oh, goody—*goody*—GOODY!" Len Maynard exclaimed as she peered through the common room window. Then she clapped her hand over her eyes. "Gosh! Isn't it blinding? If we go out, we'll have to wear our specs."

"*Shall* we go out?" Rosamund Lilley demanded as she came to see. "Will the snow be hard enough? It's only had the night, you know, to harden."

"Yes; but judging by the looks of it, I should say it got going in real earnest," Len said. She had had three winters in the Oberland now and before that, had spent a year in Canada, so she was experienced in this sort of thing.

"It *ought* to be hard enough," Alicia Landon remarked as she joined the pair. "I had a dekko at the thermometer this morning and the bottom's dropping out of it. It's away down below zero already and there's no warmth in *that* sun. It's only shining. It's a gorgeous day for ski-ing or coasting!"

"Then me for coasting! Mind out, Ros! I must go and get my sled ready!" And Len tore out of the room to seek the shed adjoining the geography room where all sleds were kept.

She was in such a hurry that she never looked where she was going and she collided with Miss o'Ryan, the history mistress, who turned the corner just as she was shooting past.

"Steady—steady!" Miss o'Ryan exclaimed with a laugh in her charming Irish voice as she caught at Len to steady her. "And where may you be going in such a hurry, my child? I thought you were supposed to *walk* down the corridors?"

"Oh, I'm awfully sorry!" Len cried. "Did I hurt you, Auntie Biddy?"

"You did not. And do remember you mayn't call me that at school. Where were you going? You answer me that."

"I was just going to see that my sled was all right. We *shall* go out this morning, shan't we? It looks marvellous from our windows."

"I see. Well, I'm telling you nothing. You must wait for the Head after prayers. You can just leave that sled of yours alone and be trotting back to your common room. No; it's no use trying any blarney. If everyone who has a sled here tries to go and see to it, a nice milling round we shall have. Be off with you!"

Foiled, Len turned and trailed back to the common room, wishing that "Auntie Biddy" wasn't quite so much on the spot. She had just reached the door when the bell rang for prayers and the girls in the room hurriedly formed into line by the door to march off in order. Jo Scott, the form prefect, was counting her flock quickly.

"Two missing—oh, you Len—and where's that idiot Yseult? Oh, *there* you are! Get into line, you two, or we'll be late for prayers. *Now* are you all ready? Then lead on, Joan." And having seen them marching out quietly, Jo tailed on behind tall Yseult, the oldest girl in the form, and they went along the corridor where the Catholics left them to go to the Speisesaal while the Protestants went on to the Hall.

Prayers always had to be taken separately, for the school, started in Tirol, had always had a goodly quota of both creeds. Mlle was responsible for the worship of the Catholics and Miss Annersley, one of the two Heads, always saw to the Protestants. Some day, they hoped to have their own little chapels, but that must be waited for at present.

Standing in the Speisesaal with the sisters who were her triplets on either side, Len forgot about her sled and joined in singing one of their favourite hymns with all her heart. In Hall, Francie was also singing, though her mood was distinctly unprayerful. Va had been marching in just as Inter V reached the lower door and, as it happened,

Virginia and Francie had gone in practically side by side.

After prayers in Hall ended, there was a minute or two's pause before the Catholics arrived to take their places with their forms. Then the Head rose from her seat where she had been chatting quietly with the mistresses on either hand, and came forward to the lectern. A sense of expectancy pervaded Hall. What was she going to say? Surely, surely they would go out this morning!

Miss Annersley smiled at them before she spoke. Then her beautiful voice brought them relief. "Yes; I know you've been tied to the house practically ever since term began. This morning, we are going to make the most of the fine weather. No lessons till after break which will be at eleven this morning. Gaudenz tells me the snow is in fine condition for both coasting and ski-ing so you may take your choice. People who want to coast, go over to the right-hand side."

There was an instant scuffle as those girls lucky enough to have their own sleds at school made for the wall. The rest sat tight and waited for instructions.

"Now," she said when quiet was restored, "when I dismiss you, you may all go and change into your sports suits. People who are ski-ing, wear your heelless boots and don't forget to bring your skis and ski-sticks. The rest, nailed boots and alpenstocks, please. *All* of you, glasses! We don't want any cases of snow-blindness if we can help it. One last word! Remember what the whistle is for and obey it instantly unless you want to go for plain walks next time." She finished with a laugh and Miss Derwent, head of the English staff, leaned forward to say in an undertone heard by all her colleagues, "Let's hope *that* threat holds them!"

The Head half-turned to give her a smile and then nodded to Miss Lawrence at the piano. The mistress swung round, struck a crashing chord and, to the tune of a lively march, they left Hall, form by form, to make for the dormitories and get into their sports suits at top speed. No one ever wasted time on an occasion like this!

The Chalet School sports suit was a cosy affair with long

trousers and windcheater in gentian blue. The ends of the trousers were well tucked down into the boots and secured firmly. A cap with ear-flaps was buttoned under the chin. A big shawl folded cornerwise was flung round the shoulders and the ends tied behind and safety-pinned to the point so that back and chest were warmly covered. Cap, shawl and the mitts which finished off the uniform were crimson and the whole was comfortable and warm-looking. They made sure that everything was in trim and then stamped off downstairs, some to collect skis and the remainder to claim their sleds.

There were four big school sleds, capable of holding six big girls or eight small ones, and these, four of the mistresses had already towed out and were piling the excited juniors on to them. Those of the prefects who were coasting, followed their example, and the entire lower school rode off in state.

About eight or nine of Inter V had their own sleds. The rest were going to ski, among them, Emerence Hope. Mary-Lou, looking round for passengers, saw her and her eyebrows mounted into her hair at the sight. She handed over her sled to Lesley Malcolm with a quick word or two and then stumped across to where Emerence was making sure that her ski-traps were safe.

"What's happened to your sled?" she asked, dire meaning in her voice.

Emerence started and reddened guiltily. "What about it?" she demanded.

"It's still here, isn't it? Why aren't you using it?"

Emerence looked positively hangdog. "Look, Mary-Lou, I've never been on the thing since—you know when, and I don't want ever to see it again."

"Rot! Of course you do!"

"No, honestly, Mary-Lou. I—I'd rather ski."

"Would you? Since when? You used to be mad on coasting."

"Well, when I think——"

"You *aren't* thinking! You're simply being morbid!" Mary-Lou told her with a firmness that admitted of no argument. "I'm not going to have it! You go and change your boots and get your alpenstock and fish out that sled pronto and no more nonsense! I told you last year I wasn't going to have any more of it and I meant it. If you don't," she wound up, "I'm going to the Head about it. This sort of thing is sheer rot! I'm perfectly fit. I've developed a little height which goodness knows I wanted, *and* my hair is curly. I did very well out of that mad accident. I'm not letting *you* lose by it, so trot off and stir your stumps or you'll keep us all waiting and more people than me will have something to say!"

"But, Mary-Lou, I——"

"Did you hear what I said? Yes, I know I'm being a nasty bully over this, but you're spoiling all your fun by this silly attitude of yours. What's more, you're spoiling mine. How do you think *I* feel when I see you acting like this?"

"Acting like *what*?" Two people had come up to them, a tiny girl, very fair and frail-looking, and one of Mary-Lou's own height who contrived to look lovely even with the disfiguring coloured glasses they all wore perched on her pretty nose.

Mary-Lou turned round. "Oh, you two! Emerence is making an owl of herself over coasting. See if you two can do anything with her. I've done *my* best, but she still clings to this insane idea that she hates it because of what happened Christmas term before last. I've warned you, Emmy."

"It isn't just that and you know it," Emerence began. But at this point, someone else came to take a hand.

Miss Ferrars, form mistress to Inter V had been told all about that affair and the attitude Emerence had taken up about coasting ever since. In fact, most of the staff had been at her that morning to do what she could with the girl. If it was allowed to go on, as Mlle had pointed out, Emerence would end up by becoming fixed in her silly morbidity and it was all wrong.

"Why are you ski-ing, Emerence?" she asked briskly. "I thought you had a wonderful sled and I'm longing to

27

see it. You never had it out last term so you must start off with it now. In fact," she added blandly, "you're taking me down on it as a beginning and I'm looking forward to it. I've done no sledging since I was about your age and I want to enjoy it again. Off you go and change. I'll wait for you. You other people get off. The rest are on the move. I'll bring Emerence along."

There was no gainsaying this. Very reluctantly, Emerence went off. The mistress waited, waving gaily to the others as they set off for the broad piece of pasture-land, running up to a fairly steep hill, which they generally used, though some of the seniors who were experienced ski-ers by this time, were allowed to go for runs much farther afield.

Emerence was quick. With "Ferry" waiting for her, she dared not linger, but when she rejoined the mistress, dragging a splendid specimen of a sled behind her, it was with a heavily clouded face. Miss Ferrars took no notice of it. She swung round beside the girl and they tramped off with the mistress chatting cheerfully and Emerence replying with monosyllables when she replied at all.

"Cheer up, Emerence!" Miss Ferrars said as they reached the foot of the hill. "You look as if you were going to be executed—or have half your teeth out at least!"

Against her will, Emerence giggled faintly, and they turned and toiled up the hill to the very top where several people were waiting their turn to go.

The last got off just as Virginia Adams came up with her small single-seater. Emerence, the clouds down again, had got her double-seater into position. Miss Ferrars gave her a quick glance. She sat down behind her pilot and clamped strong arms round the bundled-up figure in front, thus making sure that her feet were well clear of the ground.

"Give us a shove off, Virginia!" she called to that individual.

Virginia swung her sled sideways on and came to obey. She gave a rather harder push than she had intended and they went flying off down the steep slope, faster and faster as the sled gathered momentum. For the first two seconds, Emerence felt nothing but icy fear. Then the swift movement woke up something she had forced down inside her and though she had no idea she was doing it, she started yelling—a yell of sheer delight. They reached the bottom, she drew on her right rope and they came round in a fine curve, well to the side and out of the way of Virginia who had followed them.

"Gorgeous!" Miss Ferrars said, springing to her feet. "Can you give me another turn? Then I must go on duty and see what the rest are after."

Her look at Emerence was keen, but she was satisfied with what she saw. The cloud had gone. Emerence was one broad grin and the mistress knew that her foolish attitude had been broken. They went up the hill and came down with another joyous swoop and then Miss Ferrars, feeling that all would be well, thanked her pupil and went off to attend to someone else. Emerence, with the look of someone who has been wakened out of a nightmare, gathered up the ropes and began the long trail to the top of the hill down which some of the ski-ers were coming, skimming the icy surface with shouts of pleasure.

"We ought to have a proper ski-lift!" Len Maynard panted as she toiled up the slopes with her own sled, her chum, Rosamund Lilley, helping. "It *is* a drag up to the top when you have to go on your own arched insteps!"

"Jolly well worth it, though!" Rosamund laughed. "I should think it's about the nearest thing to flying that there is!"

Mary-Lou, who was sailing down the hill in grand style, Vi Lucy, Verity Carey and Barbara Chester all crammed behind her on a sled that was intended to take three at most, saw Emerence and grinned to herself.

"Ferry's done it on Emmy, thank goodness!" she shouted as she guided her sled expertly round one of the big school ones on which Elinor Pennell was taking down a bunch of juniors who were all screaming delightedly at the tops of their voices.

"Mind that sled in front!" Vi shrieked as they neared

the sled on which Francie was making a lone descent. "Right—pull *right*, Mary-Lou!"

"Right it is!" Mary-Lou hauled on the rope and they rounded Francie safely to reach the bottom where Mary-Lou wickedly went straight ahead, causing consternation among unpractised ski-ers who had to get out of her way in a hurry and as best they could. Some of them managed, others found their skis crossing and went over. But it was all part of the fun and no one minded. They were enjoying themselves too much for that!

"Isn't the air gorgeous!" Verity remarked, elevating her small nose and sniffing like a dog in covert. "It's like wine—makes you feel all revved up!"

"And how *you* know anything about the effects of wine is more than I can say." Mary-Lou remarked. "That was a good one, folks!" She swerved round and came to a full stop. "Come on! Let's have another like it!"

"Will you, indeed?" demanded a clear-cut voice behind her and she swung round to find herself facing Miss Wilson, co-Head of the school with Miss Annersley and special Head of St Mildred's, the finishing school branch. "In the first place, Mary-Lou, I'd like to point out that you've no business to come all this way. In the second—and correct me if I'm wrong!—I thought that sled of yours was built to take three people and three only? How on earth did you get *four* jammed on to it?"

"Well, one's Verity and she takes up a very tiny space," Mary-Lou said, looking as her friends did not fail to tell her later, completely dropped on.

"I daresay! You don't do it again, though. The end one might have dropped off halfway down and been run over by someone else. Oh no, Mary-Lou! We had enough of coasting accidents when Emerence laid *you* out! This school bars little luxuries of that kind. Find someone else to take one of you, you three and don't do that again, if you please."

She swung round on her skis as she spoke and skimmed away to where some people from IVb seemed to be getting into difficulties, leaving consternation behind her.

"Well, that seems to be that!" Vi said at last.

"We *would* have to barge into Bill!" Mary-Lou said disgustedly. "O.K. Let's get cracking to the top and see if we can gate-crash some lone coaster."

It seemed the only thing to do. Vi and Mary-Lou took the ropes and, with the other pair trudging behind them, they mounted to the top where they found Francie still by herself, preparing for another run.

Mary-Lou gave her a quick inquisitive look and didn't like what she saw in the lowering face. Without a moment's hesitation, she tossed her rope to Barbara.

"Hi, Francie!" she called, "wait a sec and take me. We've just been hearing remarks from—Miss Wilson on the iniquity of crowding four on to a sledge meant for three only. Vi can take that lot down and you take me, will you?"

With this, she plumped herself down behind the dismayed Francie. That young woman had decided that a good way to pay Virginia out for her interference with them would be to bump her hard. She was coasting by herself since her friends had all plumped for ski-ing, so it wouldn't affect anyone else. Virginia was just getting her sled into position and the wicked Francie, who had three winters of sports to set against Virginia's one and a bit, was quite capable of bringing it off. Mary-Lou's sudden suggestion had put a definite stop to anything of that kind. Nor did she see how she could refuse. In any case, she liked Mary-Lou as most people did.

"O.K. Come on, then!" she said, sitting down and gathering up the guide-ropes. She looked round. "Give us a shove, Betty!"

Mary-Lou settled herself and Betty Landon obliged. Off they flew, Francie wondering if she could still manage just to give Virginia a nudge accidental-done-on-purpose. Mary-Lou was famed for being on the spot, but she *might* not notice.

Vain hope! Mary-Lou *was* very much on the spot. She saw Virginia setting off and her eyes gleamed behind her dark glasses as she leapt to conclusions.

"The young *demon*!" she thought to herself. "Well, I'll ut a stop to that all right! Virginia may be far too ready to take anything and everything on herself. In fact, I should call her painfully officious! But we're having no sticky revenges from anyone if *I* can help it!"

However, her care was not needed. As it turned out, Virginia was well and truly bumped without anyone needing to do it on purpose. She was rather nervous about all winter sports and she was far from being good at any of them.

At the same time as Francie and Mary-Lou had taken off, a big school sled piloted by Miss Burnett and with a noisy selection from IIa piled on to it, had also taken off. Just ahead of these two was a small one piloted by Heather Clayton with Margot Maynard and Joan Baker as passengers. At the exact moment when Virginia was rather nervously trying to tack in order to slow herself down a little, it pleased Heather to pull sharply on her left rope so that when the sled swung across the run and Virginia with a squawk pulled on her right to avoid charging into them, Miss Burnett, coming down faster than either, since she had the weight of a half-a-dozen husky youngsters behind her, tried to pass between them and managed to avoid Heather's load by a hairsbreadth. She was not so lucky with Virginia whose inexperience was partly responsible for what happened. She *swithered*, to quote Heather later, and her sled moved first in one direction and then the other. As a result, Miss Burnett's big one caught the hinder end on the right side a glancing blow, though she contrived to keep it from being any worse. The younger girls all squealed wildly and Virginia let go her ropes—the last thing she should have done—and, as Scottish Lesley Malcolm expressed it, stotted off the thing on to the run, stotted again and finally came to rest at the side where she remained sitting with such an outraged look of surprise on her face that Mary-Lou, glancing across in time to get the full effect, nearly let go of Francie who had also seen it and was shaking with laughter.

How they ever reached the foot of the run in safety, was

something neither of them could ever explain. By the time they got there, both were screaming with mirth, and Mary-Lou rolled off the sled, gasping for breath and with tears rolling down her face at the memory.

Elinor, Sybil and Hilary, who had come skimming along to see what was happening, rushed to pick her up. They yanked her to her feet while Joan Baker did the same for Francie, hauling the light sled out of the way, and Elinor demanded: "What on earth's the matter with you two? Stop it, Mary-Lou! You'll have hysterics if you go on like that! You, too, Francie! Stop it at once, both of you!"

"Oh, *did* you see Virginia's face?" Mary-Lou gasped between her shrieks. "Did you *see* her expression? Ow! My ribs are aching!"

"We did not," Elinor said crisply. "What was wrong with it? Here, someone, find some loose snow and we'll scrub her face! Stop it, you idiot!"

Despite her struggles, Hilary and Sybil scraped some frozen snow off a handy pine-branch and rubbed her cheeks hard with it. It stopped her convulsions at least and she stood still, breathless and red-eyed behind the glasses she took off to wipe away the tears.

"*Ow!* I'm aching! Oh, dear! That was one of the funniest sights I ever saw!" She clapped on her glasses again, for the glare from the snow was blinding, and turned to Francie who looked a different girl with her habitual scowl gone and unexpected dips in her cheeks as she literally squeaked with laughter.

"Thanks a lot, Francie," she said feebly. "That was— the funniest run—I've ever had. You grab someone else while I go and make sure Virginia hasn't hurt herself. But however I'm to keep a straight face——" She was nearly off again but she caught it back in time and set off up the hill on the far side to where Virginia had got to her feet and was looking to see what had happened to her sled. It had gone quite a long way down before it came to rest at the other side and, as she was aware that quite a number of people had seen her antics, she was none too pleased.

Francie, giving a vivid account of it to her fellow

33

criminals later on that morning, wound up with, "After that, I should think she'll leave us alone for a while. She made a complete idiot of herself and quite a lot of us saw it. She jolly well ought to sing small for a bit now!"

CHAPTER FOUR

JOEY MAKES A DISCOVERY

MRS MAYNARD of Freudesheim was entertaining. It was the second Sunday of term and she had invited the two Heads, Miss Annersley and Miss Wilson, Mlle de Lachennais and Frau Mieders who were all, as she impertinently informed them, old stagers where the school came in, to take "English tea" with her and her three youngest.

The visitors had come at fifteen o'clock—three, by English time—and had had a good time playing with the four-year-old twins, Felix and Felicity, and baby Cecil who would celebrate her first birthday two months or so ahead. Now the twins had settled down to look at a big picture-book which was only allowed to them on Sunday, so was in the nature of a treat. Cecil, having just roused from her afternoon nap, was crawling about the floor with gurgles and chuckles. Crawling was her latest accomplishment and, as her mother had just observed resignedly, the only thing would be to put her into overalls, for her frocks were filthy half-an-hour after they had been put on.

"She's the most active of all my family," she said as she went to pick up the baby. "All the same, she's worse this afternoon than I've ever known her. It must be the influence of you four!"

"You cheeky brat!" Miss Wilson cried, laughing. "But then you always were!"

"Don't call me names before my offspring!" her hostess retorted. "It's a shocking example to set them. I'm surprised at you, Nell!"

"Don't you talk to me of shocking examples!" Miss Wilson flung back at her with spirit. "What about your own example? Really, Joey, for a married woman and the mother of nine you contrive to remain amazingly childish on occasion!"

Joey Maynard chuckled. "If this sort of thing is to go on it's just as well that the Coadjutor is coming to remove the infants to the play room. I can hear the fall of her fairy footsteps," she added.

The visitors went into peals of laughter, rather to the embarrassment of Rösli, known to every one as "The Coadjutor", as she came clumping into the room to collect the little ones for milk and bread-and-butter and sponge-cakes. However, she had not been nearly three years with the Maynard family without losing a good deal of her earlier shyness, so she came over to take Cecil from her mistress and hold out her free hand to little Felicity who shut the book firmly on her twin's fingers and came bundling across the room to "Wösli".

"Teatime?" their mother said with a smile. "Yes; you may take them, Rösli. I'll be up at bedtime for prayers and then you can trot off for the evening. Off you go, my sweetie-pies! Mamma will see you later on. Be good! Yes; you may say goodbye, twins."

The twins stumped round, offering kisses and drawing out the goodbyes as long as they could. Rösli waited patiently, holding a conversation with the gurgling baby in her arms. Finally, she held out her hand again.

"Come, Felicity, mein Vöglein! Felix, come with me!"

The small Maynards were well-trained. Felicity came running and Felix, after a keen look to make sure that she meant it, followed. Joey glanced across the room to the table where they had been sitting and called him back.

"Hi, Felix! What about that book? You didn't find it there. Put it in the shelf, sonny, and be quick."

"Felicity got it," Felix mentioned.

"Yes; and she closed it. It's your share to put it away. Hurry up!"

Felix did as he was told and then raced off after Rösli

and the little girls. Joey sat back with an exaggerated sigh of relief. "Thank goodness! I thought he was going to argue!"

"What a martinet!" Miss Annersley said teasingly.

"I have to be. Felix would argue the hind leg off a donkey when he's in that mood. Anyhow, as you very well know, Jack has always insisted on instant obedience. He's really far stricter about it than I am. I don't mind admitting that I *have* been coaxed on occasion; but once Jack's foot is down, it's *down*." She stood up. "Entertain each other for a few minutes, will you, while I bring tea in?—No; I don't want any help, thank you. Anna left everything ready for me and all I have to do is to bring in the whole thing when I've made the tea. Shan't be a minute!"

"Well, send Bruno in to have a word with us," Miss Wilson said. "Where is he? He generally greets us with a tail like a flail and flinging his full weight on the nearest person; but we haven't seen a hair of him this afternoon."

"Anna's gone off to visit that cousin of Rösli's who works at the hotel on the Rösleinalpe and she asked if she might take him with her." Joey paused in her flight to the kitchen, one hand on the door. "I was glad to agree because he hasn't had as much exercise as he needs lately. They're walking up by the path and will come down by train. I made Anna promise she wouldn't try to walk back—ski back, I mean. It'll be dark then and not too safe. I can hear the kettle!"

She escaped to the kitchen, and left her guests to amuse themselves.

"I wonder," Mlle said pensively, "why Joey has invited us so specially today?"

"For the sake of our company, as Jack is away in Berne, of course," Miss Annersley replied. "What other reason could she have?"

Miss Wilson had strolled over to the end window to gaze at the Jungfrau. It was a gloriously clear day and under the winter sunset the Jungfrau rose, white, austere, serene, a magnificent sight. Now she turned back into the room.

"What's eating you, Jeanne? Why *should* Joey have any special reason for inviting us? She very often does on a Sunday unless she has Jack at home."

"I know that, but," Mlle looked round at them all with sparkling black eyes full of intelligence, "I took the message and it was impressive—but *very* impressive. Therefore, I am certain she has another reason and I wish to know what it is."

"Well, with us she will be soon and then you may ask her," Frau Mieders said placidly. She was a quiet woman, rarely speaking unless she had something to say.

"Yes," Miss Wilson said emphatically. "And she will tell us just exactly when it suits her and not a moment before. For sheer aggravatingness when she chooses, I'd back Joey against anyone! Don't you ask questions, Jeanne, or she'll just sit there, standing us off and chortling to herself. I haven't known her all these years for nothing, I assure you!"

"Oh, I agree," Mlle replied demurely. "We will say nothing. Then she will tell us because she is unable to help herself."

The sound of the trolley being rolled across the parquet of the hall reached them and she jumped up to go and open the door to show Joey pushing the three-tier trolley which was the envy of many of her friends, with one hand and carrying a big covered dish in the other.

"I never knew anyone try to do so many impossibilities as you, Jo!" Miss Wilson remarked as she came striding across the room to rescue the dish. "I only wonder you haven't overturned something all over the floor!"

"Not me!" Joey retorted with great lack of grammar. "I'm accustomed to carrying goodness knows how many oddments in one hand and clutching a wriggling baby with the other. A trolley and a dish of light cakes is a mere nothing after that. Come on folks! Pull up your chairs and let's be cosy."

They gathered round, laughing and chattering in a way that would have rendered their pupils speechless with surprise if they could have been there. Joey dispensed the

37

tea and Miss Wilson handed round the light cakes which were literally swimming in butter.

"I hope you've provided soap and towels for afterwards," Miss Annersley said as she bit into hers with due care for dripping melted butter. "*Joey!* You must have used quite half-a-pound of butter on these!" She cast a mischievous glance at the plump Frau Mieders who was stolidly munching a light cake. "Anna, if you eat many of these, I'm afraid you'll add at least a pound to your weight. We three can, of course, being slender——"

"Slender? You mean skinigallees, don't you?" Joey interrupted with a giggle. "Don't you listen to her, Anna. You enjoy my hot cakes as much as you like. After all, that's what I made 'em for!"

"Did *you* make them?" Miss Wilson cried.

"I did! And no rude remarks, if you please."

"Well," observed Miss Annersley as she helped herself to another, "you may know how to cook, but I must say your English is rapidly deteriorating. Really! Joey!"

Joey grinned at her. "Thought you'd rise!" she said sweetly. "That was for *your* benefit, Hilda, and I've caught you!"

"*Hilda!*" Miss Wilson exclaimed reproachfully. "How *could* you fall for that? You ought to know what she is by this time. Joey, you're incorrigible!"

"That's an old yarn," Joey returned, quite unperturbed. "You stop calling me names and pass those light cakes round again. Or would you all rather have cream cakes? Anna was at it yesterday, too."

Miss Wilson gave her up and took one of Anna's far-famed cream cakes though she murmured after she had bitten into it, "I only hope we shan't all pay badly tonight for this afternoon's gorging!"

"Oh, Matey will cope," Joey declared airily as she pressed the plateful on her guests. "She once told me that she *always* kept castor oil handy."

"You disgusting little wretch!" Miss Annersley cried. "And while I think of it, why didn't you ask *her* if you wanted a party of old stagers—and I must say I think you

38

were needlessly rude to put it that way, Joey!—and round it off?"

"She certainly is one of us," Miss Wilson said thoughtfully. "She came half a term before I did and two terms before you, my dear. Actually, she's an older member of the school than either of us."

"So she is. I'd forgotten that." Joey poured out second cups all round and added, "As a matter of fact, I did ask her but she cried off. Said she was going to have a quiet day to herself. I thought she sounded rather—worried. Anyhow, I didn't press her. Is there anything wrong, does anyone know?"

Miss Annersley looked doubtful for a moment. Then she said slowly, "Well, we're all friends here, so I'm going to tell you that Matey had bad news on Friday. That's really why I wish she'd come instead of crying off, Joey. Her sister is desperately ill and the doctors don't give much hope for her. She's to be operated on tomorrow and it's kill or cure, I imagine, though Matey didn't actually say so. Matey is, naturally, very anxious. I offered to let her go home, but she refused. As she said, Lilian is in hospital and if—well, if she comes through, no one will be allowed to see her for some days except her husband. If she doesn't, their eldest girl is living at home since her husband's death and Eric Harper will be well looked after. She's agreed to go later if all goes well."

"But why on earth couldn't she tell me?" Joey demanded.

"I don't suppose she wants to talk about it," Miss Wilson said briefly. "She's not the kind to wear her heart on her sleeve and she won't want anyone to talk. You wait till it's over one way or the other and then see what you can do. But I'm awfully sorry to hear this, Hilda. Lilian Harper is the only relation Matey has in the world now—oh, and her family, of course—and if she goes, well, it leaves our Matey a very lonely woman. Don't go to her, Joey."

"What do you take me for? But let me know as soon as there's any news."

Joey offered a rich cake and when they were all busy with it, she changed the subject.

"I've something to tell you all," she began impressively, and Mlle looked "I told you so!" at Miss Wilson, who nodded but made no remark.

Miss Annersley was the only one who spoke and all *she* said was, "Yes?"

"We've been talking about the Dark Ages. Well, I've been thinking about them quite a lot lately." Joey stopped and looked at them all but she got no comment.

"Aren't you interested?" she demanded.

"Very!" Miss Annersley said promptly. "You go on and tell us what's worrying you. And while I think of it, why "the Dark Ages"? It was anything but that, let me tell you. Even," she wound up, "if we did have you and your little pals to cope with!"

Joey grimaced at her with a will and received a calm smile in reply. She gave it up and returned to her topic. "Do you people know what year this is?" she demanded. "I don't mean the date, but what is the important event?"

Every one hurriedly searched her mind, but no one could think of anything in particular. They gave it up after a minute.

"I can't think of a thing," Miss Wilson said frankly. "*You* tell us."

Joey finished her cup of tea and grinned fiendishly at them. "Well, you are a set of dunderheads! Don't you know what important event took place twenty-one years ago next term?"

They sat with knitted brows. Miss Wilson got there first.

"Why—wasn't that the year Madge founded the Chalet School?" she exclaimed.

"So it's dawned at last! Yes; it is. Next term, we come of age as a school."

There was an instant babel as the four mistresses commented freely.

"But me, I had not thought of it at all," Mlle said emphatically.

"Have we really been running twenty-one years? It

doesn't seem possible!" Thus Miss Annersley. "I suppose I did really know sub-consciously, but I hadn't fully realised it. Dear me! How elderly I must be growing! I was still in my twenties when I joined the school. It was my second post. My first was in a big day-school not far from my home."

"This was my *first* post," Mlle contributed. "I was barely twenty-two and oh, how afraid I was! I cried myself to sleep every night for the first week, though you may not believe it. But I knew I must make a success of it, for we were poor at home and there were six younger than I. When I think of how miserable I was—but so *miserable*! —that first week, I laugh at the silly child I was! And surely if anyone had told me then that eighteen years later I should still be teaching here and," she cast a glance at Joey, "described as 'an old stager', I should have laughed at them. It would not have seemed *possible*!"

Frau Mieders took up the story. "I came as a sad-hearted widow," she said. "I had lost my husband and my little son together and then my mother begged me to come home. I had been left poor and it seemed best to take up teaching. And so I, too, have found happiness in the so-dear school."

"Exactly!" Joey said. She paused to investigate the contents of teapot, hot-water jug and milk jug and finding them all drained, pushed the trolley to one side. " 'All gone!' as Felicity used to say. Well, here we are, five foundation stones of the school! Of *course* I'm included!" as the four mistresses raised an outcry at this. "You four may have been staff, but I was just as important. Have you forgotten that I was the very first pupil of the school? Grizel Cochrane was the second, but as she's thousands of miles away in New Zealand, she can't count in on this— or not much, anyhow. Where was I? Oh, yes! We five are among the foundation stones of the school which is why I invited you here this afternoon after I'd made the discovery what year it was. We can't let it pass, you know. We must do something to celebrate the school's coming of age next term. If we begin to consider it now, we'll have

41

practically all this term in which *to* consider it and we ought to be able to think up a few ideas by way of celebration. For one thing, we've shifted the Sale to the summer term so we ought to go all out and make it an extra magnificent event. Once the girls hear about it, they'll be all out to do everything they can. Then, not that it really has anything much to do with it, I hope you'll find you can award my special prize this year. Surely there must be someone who deserves it?"

"We'll think it over and discuss it. That's all I'll promise you," Miss Annersley told her firmly. "I won't have that prize awarded if it isn't earned, Joey."

"I could give you a name myself," Joey replied, "but I'd better not. However, I do know one girl who has been kind and helpful all round and thought of other people first and herself last over and over again."

"I suppose you mean Mary-Lou," Miss Wilson said thoughtfully. "Yes; I rather think you're right, Joey. Mary-Lou has grown into one of the best of our seniors. In fact, you may as well know at once that she's well in the running for Head Girl next year. She'll have another year in the school proper, you know, before she comes on to St Mildred's and, the way things are going, I should say there won't be any question of it. What do you say, Hilda? And you other two? Jeanne, what's your verdict?"

"But if the Margot Venables prize is to be awarded this year, unless anything exceptional chances, I would give my vote to Mary-Lou," Mlle said promptly. "She is all one could ask—kind, helpful, a steady worker and a—a good sport."

"And with that I agree," Frau Mieders' tranquil voice took up the strain.

"There you are, Hilda! That's three of us—four, if you count Joey in."

"I should just think I *do* count in!" the giver of the prize exclaimed indignantly. "It's *my* prize! Of *course*, I have a say in the matter!"

"There's nearly two terms to go yet," was all Miss Annersley would say. "I can't say anything definite yet."

42

"Well, if Mary-Lou suddenly changes right round, I— I'll eat my latest MS!" was Joey's reaction to this. "I don't think there's the least chance I shall have to keep my word about that, either," she added. "I regard Mary-Lou as one of the finest girls we've ever had. She's rock-bottom decent!"

But Miss Annersley, though she fully agreed with all that had been said, refused to commit herself further and they had to let it go at that.

"Well," the hostess observed, "there's my discovery for you."

"I suppose someone would have thought of it sooner or later," Miss Wilson said. "Like Hilda, I was vaguely aware that we must be nearing it, but I'm so busy most of the time, that I can't spare a moment for anything but my work. Still, we should have thought of it in time. Madge certainly would, if no one else."

"I suppose she might," Joey agreed as she got up to push the trolley to the far side of the room. "I don't know, though. She's awfully busy these days, what with a new house—they're still not properly settled yet—and her imps of twins; never to speak of all the society and social work she does like opening sales-of-work and garden fêtes and being president of the W.I. and chairman of half-a-dozen societies and committees and whatnots. Madge may have given up teaching finally, but she has a jolly full life of it, let me tell you! A good job, too! Do you know, folk, before she went to Canada for those two years, I'd taken to watching her in fear and trembling that she was going to develop into merely, 'that sweet woman, Lady Russell!' I saw it coming, and I'd have been mad if it had come off. There's a lot more to Madge than *that*!"

"Aber, Joey, Liebling, how scornful you sound!" Frau Mieders laughed. "Why do you so dislike a sweet woman?"

"Oh, I don't! I admire them. Mary-Lou's mother, Doris Carey, is a sweet woman and you know how fond I am of her. But there's more *to* Madge. I can't tell you how thankful I was when I got out to Canada and found her

43

brisk and crisp and snappy, just as she used to be in Tirol. She's never looked back, thank goodness!"

Miss Wilson nodded. "I agree; and I'm as glad as you. Madge has heaps of character, but I've always thought the trouble she had when Josette had that accident and then was frail for so long after rather overlaid other things."

Joey chuckled. "Nothing very frail about Josette now! And it did mean that Sybs, who seemed to be headed for becoming a most trying creature, was pulled up sharply. She's improved out of all recognition. Well, I'll remove the trolley and then we can settle down to a good thinking party; for whatever we do next term, it's got to eclipse any of our former efforts. Can't let the school come of age and just let it pass. We simply must make a real splash and all the Old Girls must be notified, too—or all those we can get into touch with," she added more soberly.

Miss Annersley gave her a quick look and changed the subject. During the war, the Chalet School had lost touch with a good many of its former members and some had gone out of reach altogether. She knew that Joey was inclined to brood over this sometimes, though usually she was too healthy-minded for that. Nothing was to be gained by letting her think of what they had lost now, so she got up from her chair and picked up the muffin dish.

"You run the trolley to the kitchen and I'll bring this. Clear those cups, Jeanne, and bring the kettle, Anna. We can't do any discussing until we've cleared the decks."

There was a bustle as they hurriedly cleared away. Then they returned to the Salon and pulled their chairs up to the great log fire Joey had burning in the open fireplace Jack Maynard had had installed when he bought the house. Cigarettes were lighted up and they put their heads together in an effort to work out something that would be good enough for the auspicious event to be celebrated next term.

CHAPTER FIVE

MISS ANNERSLEY MAKES AN ANNOUNCEMENT

"Now, Joan! Your turn! To what do you attribute the fall of Napoleon?"

Joan Baker slowly stood up, looking completely blank. Apart from the fact that she had no idea why Napoleon should have fallen as he did, she found it difficult to reason from cause to effect and she loathed these questions which Miss o'Ryan was so fond of hurling at them. Miss o'Ryan thought, and made no secret of it, that girls of fourteen and fifteen ought to be able to argue this sort of thing, even if only on the broadest lines. No one could say that she did not do her best to teach her pupils the art. Inter V loathed it. They loved the lessons during which she lectured to them, using startling metaphors and similes and any other grammatical adornment that would make her story vivid and picturesque. Most of them had begun to grasp the fact that all history is closely interwoven. Things like the French Revolution and the Peasants' Rising in the reign of Richard II did not suddenly break out, she told them, but had their roots far back in the past. Then she would delve into those earlier centuries for their benefit and prove her point to them.

That was all very well and practically all of them enjoyed it. What they did *not* like was having to work it out themselves and, in the form's opinion, she was far too fond of expecting them to do it. When she was in the mood for argument, a good many of them groaned inwardly.

Joan stood still, trying to think of something that would pass muster. Miss o'Ryan waited and then gave her a little encouragement. "Come along, Joan. Can't you think of something? Do your best."

Thus urged, Joan said, very haltingly, for her French was still very behind hand, "I think that one reason was because he wanted too much."

"Quite right! Can you go into a little more detail, though?"

"Well, he tried to conquer Russia and he lost most of the Grande Armée and got nothing by it."

"Yes?" Miss o'Ryan said as she came to a halt. "Can't you go a little further?"

Joan was dumb. She had shot her bolt. Miss o'Ryan nodded at her and she sat down with a faint sigh of relief. *That* ordeal was over!

Rosamund Lilley who came next was able to carry the argument further, making a reference to the 1812–14 Anglo-American war which drew an approving remark from the mistress. Then Len Maynard, whose favourite subject was history, created a diversion by asking if it was true that the French had mistaken the red-brick walls of the old farmhouse at Quatre Bras for the red coats of the British and wasted a lot of ammunition firing at them and if that had not had something to do with the Allies' victory at Waterloo?

"Well, from all accounts, by the time the engagement was over, the whole place was a shambles," Miss o'Ryan agreed while the rest of the form waited breathlessly to see if she would really follow the red herring Len had so guilelessly drawn across her path or if she would ignore it and go on with her questioning.

She went on. "At the same time, don't forget that if the French wasted men and ammunition there, our army was poor. Do any of you know what Wellington said about it?"

No one did, so she obligingly gave them the quotation from Wellington's letter to Lord Stewart: "I have an infamous army; very weak, and ill-equipped, and a very inexperienced staff."

The girls exclaimed and she added to their horror.

"Apart from that," she said, "not only were the Government at home disgracefully niggardly with supplies while the men and officers were often only part-trained. The discipline in some divisions was none too good. After the battle was over, Wellington complained that both officers and men were absent from their posts without leave and

46

that they were spreading false alarms throughout the country in a way he describes as 'highly unmilitary and derogatory to the characters of soldiers.' " She added, "It was an outrageous thing and if the discipline had been what it ought to have been, such a thing could never have happened."

"Then how on earth did we manage to win?" Emerence Hope asked curiously.

"I think," Miss o'Ryan said slowly, "that we won because once he is in the thick of battle, the British soldier doesn't know how to spell the word "defeat". Even when things were at their worst so that some of the commanding officers thought that all was lost, the battered regiments formed up again and came streaming back to take more punishment—and give it. It was a question of which could take the worst beating. The French were all dash and fire; but their losses were awful; even worse than ours. Finally, the crack regiment, Les Gardes Impériales, broke before the storm of fire that was enfilading their ranks as well as facing them and that was the beginning of the end. Frenchmen everywhere regarded Les Gardes as invincible and when cry sounded, 'The Guards break!' the other regiments which had been very badly decimated, anyhow, simply threw in their hands. The cost to the allies was enormous, but it brought the end of Napoleon and his attempt at world domination."

The bell rang for the end of the lesson and she stopped there. She dictated their homework and then added, "After Break, every one is to go to Hall. Miss Annersley has something to say to you—something very important, too," she concluded, wickedness gleaming in her deeply-blue Irish eyes as there came an excited stir among the girls. "Line up for your elevenses, please. Jo, lead them to the Speisesaal and don't waste time."

Then she fled to escape questioning and Inter V were left to surmise what was in the wind now, which they did at once. Jo Scott, as form prefect, sat heavily on their chatter, however.

"Stop *talking*!" she ordered. "Form up at the door,

47

please! Do you *want* a word with Karen for being late for cocoa and biscuits? Line up, and don't be silly!"

The girls stopped talking at once and lined up. During the previous term, there had been bad trouble among them and the Head had finally brought them to heel by announcing that unless they reformed, their form title should be changed and they would be included among the middles instead of the seniors. No one wanted *that* disgrace and they mostly did their best not to earn it. Now, headed by Jo, they marched off to the Speisesaal where Karen, head of the domestic staff at the school, was waiting to dispense cocoa or hot milk and lemon biscuits of her own making. Karen was universally pronounced "a complete pet" by most of the school, but she had a temper and they were wise enough not to try to rouse it.

Once they had finished their elevenses, Inter V streamed off to their common room, since the weather was much too bad for going out, and made up for lost time so far as their French would let them. It is only fair to say that most of them were fairly well off for vocabulary, but it is to be feared that a really good French accent was far to seek in many cases.

"What *can* the Head want with us?" Rosamund Lilley demanded of her own special coterie when they had gathered in a corner.

"You know as much as I do," Jo Scott replied, hooking a chair to her with one foot and sitting down. "Perhaps it's to settle which of us are wanted for speaking parts in the St Mildred's panto. So far, it's only the kids for chorus and ballet they've chosen. We've heard about nothing else so far."

"They're leaving it awfully late, aren't they?" Len Maynard said, balancing on the arm of Jo's chair. "D'you know, you folk, I'm very disappointed."

"Because they've left it so late do you mean?" Jo asked, looking startled.

"Of course not! That's *their* affair. No; I mean they've had *different* pantos up to this. They've done *The Sleeping Beauty* and then *Beauty and the Beast* and *The Willow*

48

Pattern. It's rather a come-down when they pitch on just *Aladdin*."

Thanks to a year spent in Canada during which she and her sisters had attended a French convent school as boarders, Len's own French was excellent—even idiomatic; and her accent and intonation were as French as Mlle's. As for her use of French slang, she frequently left her elders gasping. The second term at La Sagesse had been spent entirely there, for the Maynard twins were only a week old when term began and every one had united in insisting that with twin babies and her two younger boys, Charles and Michael, Joey had enough on her hands without the additional worry of the triplets and Stephen, the eldest boy. The three were excellent mimics and very musical and they had come home at Christmas thorough little Frenchwomen in tongue, at any rate. Nor had any of them lost it. Christmas holidays are brief in Canada and they had been at La Sagesse for the whole of the Easter term. Their mother, rejoicing in the fact that they were quickly becoming bilingual, had insisted that only French be spoken at home until they returned to England and, as a result, Len and her sisters could speak with a fluency so far not attained by anyone else in their form. Oddly enough, Inter V was made up of British girls only, whereas all the other forms had at least one Continental and some of them as many as half-a-dozen.

"If they make *Aladdin* as pretty as they did *The Willow Pattern*, it'll be well worth seeing," Alicia Leonard remarked. "I did enjoy that! And it was awfully funny, as well."

"Perhaps they don't need us this time." It was Emerence Hope who made this suggestion.

"They're having some of us for chorus and ballet," Len pointed out.

"Yes; but I meant *speaking* parts. They've got quite a lot of girls at St Mildred's this year, haven't they?"

"They'll have to have Verity Carey, anyhow," Margot Maynard stated positively. "They haven't anyone there to touch her when it comes to singing."

"Verity can sing, but she can't act for toffee!" Emerence said, tempting providence by speaking in English.

"She was quite good as the 'Fairy Queen' last year," Con Maynard said thoughtfully.

"Oh, pooh! Not much acting in that! All she had to do—mostly, anyhow—was to move about gracefully and sing and look pretty. Not much acting needed there," Jo pointed out. "Not for Verity, anyhow. She *is* awfully pretty with that mane of fair curls and her lovely eyes. And when she moves, she always makes me think of a bird flitting along."

There was no time for more, for the bell rang for the end of Break and they had to stop talking, line up, and march to Hall. Discipline was good at the Chalet School and even if it hadn't been, the prefects were in Hall in full force so they took their seats in silence. On the whole, if they *had* to get into trouble, most of them preferred it to be with the staff rather than the prefects!

Len settled herself comfortably and looked round. No mistress had arrived yet, but the school was very quiet and orderly on the long green forms that filled about half of Hall. Outside, the snow was falling, not in a mad blizzard as it had done at the beginning of term, but with a steadiness that meant it had no idea of stopping just yet. Probably, Len reflected, it would go on all day. Oh, well, this was the second week in February. Soon they would be into March and then they could look forward to the thaws; and decent weather, once they were over.

"Anyway," she said to herself with a silent chuckle, "we're missing arithmetic. There won't be much time for anything like that by the time the Head's arrived and told us why she wants us. That's so much to the good!"

Like her mother before her, Len was no mathematician and anything that helped to cut out any branch of that hated subject was welcomed by her with open arms.

At the other end of the long line of Inter V sat Yseult Pertwee who was thinking very much the same thing. She deeply resented having had to come to this school from one where artistic subjects were made the principal ends of

50

school life. At the Chalet School, while the arts had their place, only highly gifted girls were given extra time in them and then only when they had reached a certain standard in their general education. Yseult fancied herself as an elocutionist, but her ordinary work was so far behind what it should have been, that no one would listen for a moment when she asked to be allowed to specialise. She was two years too old for her present form and the Maynard trio were actually three years younger than she, but it was as high as she could be placed in the school, Inter V being the last—and newest—of the senior forms.

Mrs Pertwee was in America, lecturing in various places on the Arthurian legends and the three Pertwee girls had spent their Christmas holidays at Penny Rest, a charming Cornish guest-house which catered for young people. From there, Yseult had written almost frantically to her mother, begging to be taken away from the school. Mrs Pertwee was a weak-minded parent when her "girlies" were with her; but miles apart from them, she managed to be strong and, apart from that, she was enjoying herself far too much to want to have to drag a girl of nearly seventeen about with her everywhere. She felt that for nearly eleven years she had devoted herself entirely to her family and she was revelling in this taste of freedom from such responsibilities. Her reply to Yseult had been that eighteen was quite old enough to leave school and the girl must resign herself to that fact.

"Mother knows how much her big girlie wants to give more time to her verse-speaking and acting," she had written, "but really pet, your work is so poor in other subjects that I feel I must stiffen my upper lip and be *firm*. So the answer is no; not until you are eighteen."

The rest of the letter had nothing to do with this story, but this paragraph had made the recipient rage. She had no one to whom she could go for sympathy. Her two younger sisters, Véronique and Valencia, known, as Mary-Lou had once remarked, to their fellow criminals as Ronny and Val, were enjoying life at the school up to the hilt and merely stared at her when she said something

51

of what she thought to them. It was no use saying anything at school itself. The other girls quite frankly thought
her idiotic and some of them would never have spared to
say so. All she could do was to try to feel superior, but it
didn't give her much comfort.

The door at the top of the room opened and Miss
Annersley swept in, complete in M.A. gown and hood.
After her came Miss Wilson, also gowned and hooded, and
the school sat up and took notice. What was going to
happen now? It was well-known that neither mistress was
given to wearing what the school at large called "full
regalia" unless during teaching hours or for formal
occasions. Quite a number of them had met Miss Annersley
before Break when she had been wearing only her black
skirt and crimson twin set. She did no teaching that
morning, either, so why was she got up like this?

The two Heads made their way to the dais and the
school, which had promptly risen at their entrance, stood
waiting and wondering.

"You may sit down, girls," Miss Annersley said, her
beautiful, deep voice reaching to the farthest end of Hall,
though she had not raised it at all.

The girls sat down and there was a little stir of expectancy as she came to lean on the lectern and began to speak.

"I have something very important to tell you people,"
she began, speaking in English so that the most single-
tongued of the girls might understand. "It is this. Next term,
this school comes of age. Twenty-one years ago in April,
Madame—Miss Bettany in those days—opened the Chalet
School in the original chalet on the shore of the Tiernsee,
the loveliest lake in Tirol." She stopped and smiled at her
pupils. They smiled back, but a good many brains were
working furiously.

Miss Annersley gave them no chance to give tongue to
their thoughts. She went on swiftly: "Naturally, we must
celebrate. The thing is, what can we do to make our celebrations worthy of such an event? I am going to tell you of
some ideas we have already had. First we are going to
take you in parties to see the place where we began and to

learn to know some of the walks and so on that we loved so dearly when the school was *very* young. Not all are possible, I'm afraid. The walk by the lakeside was becoming none too safe, even in our time, and now it has been closed and one made further up the slope. But others are very much the same. So we are dividing you up into four parties —seniors, senior middles, junior middles and juniors— and each will spend a long weekend up there at one of the hotels of which there are several in Briesau, the chief village by the lake."

She paused there and the girls broke into rapturous clapping. They had all heard plenty about the Tiernsee and now they were to see it at last! They approved of this part of the celebrations whole-heartedly. She gave them their heads for a minute or so before she took up her tale again. Then she held up her hand and silence fell at once. The school was anxious to hear what more was to come.

"Then there will be our annual Sale as we have moved it to the summer term," she said. "We must all work hard to make it the best we have ever had. We propose to link it with another fruit and flower show like the one we had the summer before last. Mrs Maynard who, as Joey Bettany, was the very first pupil the school had, is throwing open her garden for the purpose. Besides that, she insists that her own special prize, the Margot Venables prize, shall be awarded this year. Furthermore, she is going to double its value on this occasion."

This time, the girls cheered. Joey Maynard's own schooldays might be years behind her, but she was still regarded as an integral part of the school and they all loved her—except Yseult who had closed up before even her charm, mainly because everyone else thought so much of her.

This time, the two Heads laughed outright and Miss Wilson came to stand by her colleague and help to hush the noise for the excited girls were well away. When they were sitting quietly again, she took up the story.

"Yes; well we're very glad to know you all approve so highly of this. I hope every last girl of you is going to do her best to win it. Even the babiest of all the juniors has a chance of that, you know. You needn't be a prefect to be kind and helpful on all occasions, putting others first and yourself last. And that's what the Margot Venables prize is given for. And here's something else for you. We intend to institute a Reunion Day when we hope as many of the Old Girls and mistresses as possible will join us. As this is the coming of age year and we are just making a start, it will be a Reunion Weekend to give it a good send-off."

"Oh, *marvellous*!" Len Maynard was heard to murmur, though no one took any notice of her. They were too busy cheering again.

"And now," Miss Wilson resumed when at last they had calmed down again, "you girls ought to have some ideas to add to ours. You are all to think hard for the next week and see what you can propose to add to our celebrations. This is Tuesday. Exactly a week today, the voting boxes will be set up in the entrance hall and if you have any ideas, write them on slips of paper *without* adding your names, and drop the slips into the boxes. I promise you on behalf of us all that every single slip will be read and carefully considered. And that brings me to an important point. Please will any would-be jokers leave the boxes alone! We haven't time to waste over 'funny' ideas. And another thing, remember that it all has to take place in the summer term so it's no use suggesting ski-ing or snow-balling or anything like that. Finally, try to realise that none of us are millionaires, so don't offer us any wildly extravagant suggestions for they won't be considered.

"And now," she went on in an entirely different tone, "I have something else to say to you. This year, St Mildred's is a full house so we shan't need any help from any of you but Verity Carey. Verity, we want your voice so I hope you'll help us."

Verity, very small and slim, went scarlet at this public notice, but replied in the silvery voice that matched her appearance so perfectly. "Yes, of course, Miss Wilson. I'll do everything I can."

"Good! Then I'll put Julie Lucy on to you. She is producing for us this year." Miss Wilson smiled at Verity and went on to the general public. "We hope you won't be too disappointed, girls, but we really don't need you for special parts this time. I thought I'd break the news to you myself in good time so that you can get over your disappointment. So that will be chorus, ballet, the orchestra and Verity. The rest of you! We expect to be using Hall three evenings in the week. Please keep out! The doors will be locked, once we are all assembled, but don't come trotting along and trying to come in for any reason whatsoever—unless, of course, the place is on fire," she added as an afterthought. "Anyone who is caught doing so will be prosecuted with the utmost rigour of the law. The law will be in the hands of Julie and Co." She gave them all a wide grin and they grinned back at her rather uncertainly. She knew and they knew that after that warning it would be a very daring person who braved Julie Lucy and her crowd. She went on serenely. "Well, I think that's all either of us has to say to you, isn't it Miss Annersley?"

"Only that if anyone has any questions to ask we'd be glad to answer them—so far as we can," Miss Annersley said prudently. "This will be your only chance, so ask them now."

At least ten hands shot up as she finished. She smiled down at small Ailie Russell who had been first and asked, "Yes, Ailie?"

"Please, I only want to know if Mummy will be coming?" Ailie said.

"We hope so. We want her for as long as possible," the Head said while Ailie's elder sisters, Sybil and Josette, squirmed and Josette muttered to her next-door neighbour, "Oh, for goodness sake! Why couldn't she tell the kid to put a sock in it?"

Mary-Lou had jumped to her feet. "When shall we know which suggestions have been accepted?" she asked. "This is February and some of them may need quite a lot of preparation."

Miss Annersley hesitated and glanced at her co-Head

before replying. "I'm afraid I can't tell you that at once, Mary-Lou. Probably in about a week. You must give us time to consider everything, you know. You shall hear as soon as we can manage it, though."

"I see. Thank you. It's only that half-term will be just about a fortnight away."

"There," said Miss Wilson, coming to the rescue. "You're a little out in your reckoning, my child. Easter comes late this year—the middle of April. Half-term is the second weekend in March. That's nearly a month ahead."

Mary-Lou thanked her and sat down composedly. Miss Annersley came forward. She had thought of something else. "Before I forget," she said, "please write clearly. Your idea may be a very good one, but if it is written illegibly, we shan't bother with it. We have far too much to do to waste time trying to solve enigmas!"

"I quite agree!" This was Miss Wilson. "So don't say you haven't been well and truly warned!" she added, laughing.

The girls joined in her laughter and then Elinor Pennell was on her feet.

"I should like to ask if we seniors can help with letting the Old Girls know," she said. "There must be hundreds of them. Some of us know quite a number. If we sorted them out among ourselves wouldn't that be rather a help?"

"Good for you, Elinor!" Miss Annersley exclaimed. "That's an excellent idea. We shall, of course, have a printed notice sent round, but if some of you girls care to send personal letters with them, enlarging on the notices we may have more chance of gathering in our hundreds. Also it will save Miss Dene's time—which is pretty full already. I'll let you know when the notices come and anyone who wants to help may come to the office and ask for them. We should like as many of the Old Girls and former mistresses as we can persuade to come."

"Where *will* they all stay?" Hilary Bennet asked.

Miss Wilson replied to that. "Well, we are clearing out of St Mildred's for one thing. All the St Mildred girls are coming back here. For another, Mrs Maynard has offered to crowd in as many as she can and so have other people up here. We'll manage somehow or other—if we have to pitch the Guide tents in the gardens to help out!" she concluded. "It will be only for the one weekend. Anyone else who wants to stay on after that must find rooms in the nearest hotel."

That seemed to end the questions, though several people with an eye to the next lesson which was not to their taste, tried wildly to think of something that would delay them a little longer. No one succeeded. The whole idea had been sprung on them so suddenly that, as Len said indignantly, it made their minds a blank. After giving them a minute or so, Miss Annersley called on Nina Rutherford to come and play them out and they had to go, most of them feeling far too excited to worry about algebra or the ocean currents or French idioms.

This, the Heads had expected and had made their arrangements with the staff accordingly. As a result, when they reached their form rooms, they all discovered their form mistress awaiting them and the next lesson for everyone was dictation—French dictée, in the case of VIa and English dictation for the rest. A very lengthy dictation it was, too, keeping them hard at it and giving them a chance to calm down a little. That it was badly needed was evident when the mistresses brought the finished sheets to the two Heads.

"Dear me!" Miss Wilson said rather blankly as she regarded the wild spelling from members of even Va. "Is it natural lack of spelling ability, excitement, or bad teaching on our part? I'd no idea this school contained so many appalling spellers!"

CHAPTER SIX

INTER V DISCUSS THE QUESTION

"I WONDER," said Heather Clayton pensively when they were all hard at work that evening during the weekly Hobbies Club session, "if they will agree that we are seniors enough to be counted in among those who write to the Old Girls?"

The Head had been merciful and given permission for them to talk in any language they chose during hobbies and they were all making the most of the permission.

"If I don't," Miss Annersley said to the assembled staff when she told them her decision, "they'll probably all burst from either suppressed excitement or spontaneous combustion! Either way would be tiresome! So let the prefects know, will you? We may as well let them get the worst out of their systems as quickly as possible!"

Hence the positive buzz of chatter in Inter V who, as seniors, might work alone in their common room so long as they didn't make too much of a riot.

"I don't see why not," Betty Landon returned in answer to Heather's remark. She paused to match up her embroidery silk and thread her needle. Then she went on, "After all, we *are* seniors now and some of us have been at the school since St Briavel days. I was, myself. I can think of two or three Old Girls I could write to—Edris Young for one. She lives not far from us and I often see her in the hols. She's training as a nurse, you know."

"I'm writing to Auntie Daisy." Len Maynard announced, looking up from her treadle fretsaw where she was cutting out jigsaw puzzles. She laid a piece on the little pile in a box and readjusted her wood while she went on. "I'm going to tell her to come and bring her baby, Tony, with her. Mamma would be thrilled to have her and I'm dying to see Tony."

"Mother's prob'ly writing to her herself," Margot put in as she finished cutting out a delicate wreath of buttercups and daisies from a sheet of wallpaper and handed it over to Emerence. "There you are, Emmy. I should think it'd just go nicely round that oval picture you've stuck in the middle of the page."

"Good-oh!" Emerence lifted it and fitted it round the said oval to make sure before she began to paste. "It's a bonza frame and that looked so bare."

"I expect she is," Len said, referring to her sister's first remark. "All the same, I think it 'ud be a good idea to write from the school as well."

"I'm going to write to Auntie Rob," Con observed, pausing for a moment in her hemming of a baby's nightdress.

"What's the good of that? You *know* she can't come!" Margot exclaimed.

"Why ever not?" asked Rosamund Lilley in surprise. This was her third term at school but she had only heard incidentally about "Auntie Rob".

"Because she's a nun, of course. She's teaching in the same convent in Toronto where we three went to school when we were there," Margot explained amiably. "Nuns can't do as they like, you know. They've got to do what Reverend Mother says."

"All the same, I'm writing," Con repeated, quite unperturbed by this. "She's an Old Girl, just like everyone else, so she has a right to be asked. I know she won't come, all right, but she'd hate it if she was left out—'specially when she's nearly as old an Old Girl as Mamma. She came to the school when it was in Tirol."

"And that," Margot put in, "was before we three were born!"

"Ages and ages before," Len agreed, finishing her puzzle and looking round for the box to hold it.

"It's behind you," Alicia Leonard said.

"I'd like to do something that would make us stand out as a form," Heather said. "We're a Fifth form, but it's a new kind of Fifth and some of the seniors, especially in Va, have been frightfully snooty about us, looking down their noses at us and all that kind of thing. Can't we do something to show them they're all wrong and we're as good as they are?"

"Better keep out of rows this term then," someone said with point and the rest giggled whole-heartedly. If she *could* get into trouble, Heather did!

Heather herself joined in the giggles. "Don't worry! Dad had a few things to say about my general report at

Christmas and I had to promise I'd pull up. What I meant, anyhow, was can't we do something *startling*?"

"Such as what?" Jo demanded.

But there, Heather's ideas wilted. "Oh, I don't know," she said vaguely. "Something like—well, like doing a pageant on our own——"

"We couldn't; there aren't enough of us," Alicia pointed out.

"I've thought of something." Rosamund was flushed with the effort of speaking.

"Speak now, then, or forever hold your peace! What is it?" Betty asked.

"Well, someone was telling me that we're to have a fresh piece of the garden given to us, now we've taken more in," Rosamund said. "Couldn't we go all out and make it the best part of the lot. It's the new part—virgin soil—so we ought to be able to do a lot with it."

"We'll have to do a lot of weeding," Jo grinned. "Are you sure we're to have some of the new, Ros? Who told you?"

"Vi Lucy. She and some of that gang have bagged a biggish piece and ours comes next. Vi said they meant to turn theirs into a rose garden and she hoped we'd leave the roses to them and concentrate on something else. I said I thought that would be O.K. There's plenty we can grow without having roses and they do need an awful lot of attention. Couldn't we make ours into a herbaceous garden——"

"Only herbs? I call that frightfully dull!" Betty remarked.

Rosamund broke into a peal of laughter. "Oh, Betty! "Herbaceous" hasn't anything to do with *herbs*! It means things like pansies and pinks and marigolds and——"

"Wey! Stop there! We don't want a whole catalogue of flowers!" Francie Wilford cried with a broad grin. "We get you—*flowers*! It's an idea, chaps, isn't it? We might make ourselves into groups of say three each and each group take one or two kinds and be responsible for them."

"Then bags me pansies and stocks!" Len cried. "Would

your dad get the plants for us, Rosamund? He'd probably know which would do best up here."

"Oh, rather! He'd be awfully keen. You choose what you want to grow and I'll write and tell him and then in the hols he'll get the plants collected up. We'll have to have plants this year, but another, I vote we grow our own from seed. That's the *right* way to do it."

"We could have it looking a picture for the Reunion Weekend," Jo mused aloud.

"Then we'll all have to pitch in like mad, once the snow goes and the ground's dried out enough," remarked Iris Woodley, whose own father was a keen gardener in his spare time.

"We can't do anything until the men have dug it over for us," Rosamund said.

"Oh, well, they'll do that in the hols," Len observed. "What *I* would like to do," she went on as she finished choosing her next puzzle from the little pile of wood with pictures glued to it which she had ready, "is get up a form magazine for the occasion."

"We'll have a special number of *The Chaletian*—sure to!" Francie exclaimed.

"I know that. What I meant was an Inter V mag., with stories and poems and things like that from ourselves only."

Yseult had been considering while the rest talked. Now she suddenly spoke. "We certainly couldn't manage a pageant—Alicia's right there. You need whole crowds to do anything worth while. But we might do one or two one-act plays and I could produce. I've done a lot of acting."

"But there's nothing new about that. We often get up plays on Saturday nights as it is," Francie objected.

"Oh, I didn't mean those childish things—*Scenes from Little Women*!" Yseult said with disdain, "or *Scenes from Nicholas Nickleby*! Though it might be rather good if we had *one* written by ourselves. I could——"

What she was going to say was lost in Betty's shout. "Oh, Con! That sort of thing is right up your street!"

Con looked dubious. Her great ambition at present was

to be a poet and so far, she had not tackled a play. "D'you think I could?" she asked doubtfully.

"Of course you could! Doesn't your own mother write plays—and your aunt?" Emerence cried. "And you *can* write poetry. You could do us a play in verse!"

"Well, I might have a shot," Con conceded. "It ought to be easier in verse. What sort of a play would you want, anyhow?"

"Something that wouldn't need too many fancy dresses," remarked someone at the far end of the table. "We shan't have much time for sewing things like that."

"No; that's true," Len said. "Best stick to something we can use drapery things for. You couldn't exactly do a poetry play for today."

At this point, Yseult broke in again. It was *her* suggestion and she had no idea of letting the entire form take charge of it as they showed every sign of doing. "As I proposed it and I shall produce it, I think the choice of play should be mine," she said, annoyance rampant in her voice. "I do *not* intend to waste my time on the sort of thing a mere child like Con could write."

Margot's blue eyes suddenly gleamed. "Well, what *do* you propose, then?" she demanded.

"For one thing, I should like us to do Yeats' play, *The Land of Heart's Desire*," Yseult replied, sublimely ignorant of the fact that even grown-ups might blanch at the idea of producing anything so difficult with its eerie atmosphere. "Then, I meant to write a short sketch myself— something modern, to form a contrast. You Maynard girls aren't the only ones with a mother who writes!"

"No; but they're the only ones with a mother who writes books we're allowed to have in the library," Francie retorted before anyone could stop her. "Miss Derwent turned anything of *your* mother's down when Mary-Lou asked if we ought to have one of her books for the senior library."

Yseult gave a superior smile. "Mrs Maynard writes school stories and books for children. My mother writes novels."

"And so does Godmother!" Jo Scott riposted. "Hers are all in the library here." She forgot for once that she was form prefect and supposed to keep order. Yseult always riled her as she did so many of them. Therefore, Jo added with an innocent air, "Of course, Godmother's books are very well written. I've heard people say her English is really beautiful."

Yseult flushed, but before she could retort back, the door opened and their form mistress came in to see how they were getting on.

Miss Ferrars—"Ferry" to the girls in private—was quite young. This was her first post and during the previous term she had had a little difficulty in finding her feet. She had managed it by the end of term and now she was a great favourite with the girls, especially her own form. They liked her crisp way of dealing with them and, while they admired her and enjoyed the friendliness she showed them out of school hours, they remained in sufficient awe of her to take no liberties with her.

As Miss Dene, the school's secretary, had once said, she had plenty in her favour. She was always trim and smart and, without being pretty, she was very attractive-looking. She was willing to listen to the girls' side of a question and they had always found her strictly just. Further, when the summer term came, they were to find her a fine tennis-player and keen on cricket into the bargain. She taught her own subjects—junior maths and geography—with an enthusiasm that helped them to appreciate something of what she was trying to teach them and her language was vivid and picturesque which was helpful in geography. You can't be picturesque in algebra or geometry!

When they saw her, the girls jumped to their feet and welcomed her delightedly.

"Do come and tell me which you think would be the best centre for this facing page in my scrap-book, Miss Ferrars," Emerence implored her. "I've a girl's head here, you see. Would you put this man's? Or do you think the rearing horse?"

"But how very pretty, Emerence!" Miss Ferrars exclaimed as she gave her mind to it. "I do like that wreath you've put round the girl's head! Oh, I think I'd have the man—and put another wreath round him. Save the horse for another page."

She went the rounds, admiring, commenting, and giving advice when it was asked. "Hobbies" belonged to the girls and no mistress ever interfered unless asked to do so. She complimented Yseult on her beautiful embroidery and Con on her dainty hemming, and admired Len's jigsaw of frolicking kittens, declaring her intention of buying one of the said jigsaws at the Sale.

"You'd better have one of Mamma's," Len said. "They're heaps bigger than mine. Mine only run to one or two hundred pieces but hers are eight or nine."

"She taught Len how to cut puzzles," Margot remarked. "And she gave her that treadle fretsaw for Christmas. She can't spare hers, she says."

Miss Ferrars had seen one or two of the big puzzles for which Mrs Maynard was famous in the school. She laughed at Len. "All the same, Len, I must have something from each of my pupils. I want a set of those raffia dinner-mats, Francie; and one of Len's jigsaws; and a scrap-book from Emerence for the Cottage Hospital at home—in fact, when the time comes, I'm buying first from you. What I have left after that may go to the rest." She finished her rounds and left them because a message from Miss Dene called her to the telephone.

Inter V settled down, cheered enormously by her visit, and then Emerence, who was nothing if not persistent, demanded to know why Yseult imagined that *she* should be the only one to have any say in the matter of a play?

"Well," Yseult began, "if I'm to produce it——"

"Who said you were?" Francie demanded. "We'll have to vote on that." She added in all too audible tones as an aside, "I know who my vote *won't* go to!"

"Oh, indeed!" Yseult most unwisely took it up. "And why not, pray?"

Francie gave her a blank stare. "What are you talking about?"

64

"Oh, I heard what you said! Don't imagine I didn't!" Yseult was furious and for once she forgot her dignity and descended to the level of a member of Lower Fourth. "I'm not going to be treated like that, either! How dare you say such things about me? Why shouldn't I produce? I should say I'm the only girl in the form capable of doing it!"

"We've only *your* word for that," Francie told her with maddening calm.

"Stop scrapping, you two!" Jo Scott entered the field. "As for the play, if we do one, the person to decide about it will be Ferry, *I* should have thought. She's our form mistress, in case you've forgotten it. We can't do a thing about it until we've consulted her. Now let it alone and talk about something else!"

Yseult was so thoroughly roused that she might have retorted to this, but Len Maynard got in first. "Anyway, a play for just us isn't something to help with the school celebrations and that's what we were talking about. And I *believe*," she added, "that I've got just the teeniest, weeniest speck of an idea that will be for the whole school."

"Oh, what is it?" half-a-dozen voices demanded at once.

Len shook her head until her chestnut pigtails flew. "Not going to talk about it yet. I must think it out—and I'd like some advice from someone grown-up. But if we *could* manage to do it, it would be simply *marvellous*!"

She stuck to that, though almost everyone teased for at least a hint. To all queries, she sat there, working hard at her jigsaw and smiling to herself in a way that was simply maddening to her own clan. Only her triplet sisters ceased to bother her after the first. First Con exclaimed, "*Oh*!" and then sat with wide dark-brown eyes looking as if they saw visions. Then Margot suddenly flushed with excitement and she raised the black eyebrows, which were so oddly at variance with her golden hair and roses-and-lilies skin, at Len who nodded as if she understood. After that, the pair attended strictly to their work and Emerence after murmuring to Margot, "Tell me later, Meg, won't you?" also became absorbed in her scrap-book. Yseult, of course was asking no questions of anyone. She sat working at her embroidery, her eyebrows drawn together in a scowl that might have graced Francie Wilford's face on occasion.

At length they gave it up and, for the remainder of hobbies, talked more or less idle chatter. Miss Ferrars arrived towards the end to oversee the clearing away and Con, who was given to putting into words things the rest would have left unsaid, smiled at her as she came in and said dreamily, "You come pat upon your call, Miss Ferrars."

Miss Ferrars looked startled. "What's that, Con? What are you talking about?"

"We've been discussing what the Head said this morning," Con said placidly. "We've been thinking out things to do next term to celebrate. Do you think that we—all of us Inter V, I mean—could give a play to the others? And if so, do we choose it or do you? And who's to produce?"

Well! Not for the first time since they had known her, a good many of Con's little playmates wished viciously that they could smother her! Why on earth could she never hold her tongue? Or if she *must* talk, why couldn't she put things a little less baldly?

Miss Ferrars sat down on the edge of the nearest table and looked round. "What is all this in aid of?"

Jo decided swiftly that she had better explain before Con could get going again or goodness only knew what she might say next! Jo was old enough to realise that the sort of squabble that had gone on between Francie and Yseult was hardly the sort of thing to be expected among seniors. She spoke up quickly.

"We were talking about what we could do towards the celebrations next term—as a form, I mean," she explained. "Yseult was wondering if we could give a play."

"Not at all a bad idea," Miss Ferrars assented. "What sort of a play do you think of doing?"

"Couldn't Con write one?" Betty asked eagerly. "She's miles and away the best of us all at that sort of thing and she *can* write poetry, so doing a play ought to be easy to her."

66

"I wouldn't say that," Miss Ferrars spoke thoughtfully. "When do you want to give it—and to whom?"

"Oh, just to the school, of course!" Con had lost her dreaminess and was very much on the spot for once. "I couldn't possibly write anything good enough for outsiders to come to!"

Yseult threw her a scornful look. "That wasn't what I meant at all, Miss Ferrars. I thought we might get up perhaps three one-act plays and invite people to come and see them and have a silver collection for the free ward. It would all add to the sum we hope to collect for the Sanatorium."

Miss Ferrars surveyed them with something in her brown eyes that they didn't understand. "If you like to get up *one* sketch and give it as one of the entertainments at the Sale, I see no reason why you shouldn't," she said in judicial tones. "It mustn't require too much dressing and it must have enough parts. If Con—or Con with two or three assistants—can also *write* the play, it would be an additional attraction. But I'm afraid your suggestion as it stands is rather too much on the ambitious side, Yseult. It would mean a lot of rehearsing and I doubt if you'd have time for it. What play had you thought of yourself?"

"*The Land of Heart's Desire*," Yseult said promptly.

"*What*?" Miss Ferrars exclaimed. "But my dear girl, you couldn't touch it! It's far too difficult for schoolgirls! To start with, there isn't one of you who could play Mary Bruin. And it depends tremendously on its eeriness which you couldn't hope to produce! Oh no, Yseult! That won't do at all!"

Yseult flushed and her eyes sparkled angrily, but she said no more. In the face of Miss Ferrars' downright remarks, she could hardly do so. But she thought to herself that *she* could have played Mary Bruin. She had seen it once and had been tremendously taken with the part. The rest rushed in with a clamour for Con to write a play for them.

"And you'll produce it for us, won't you, Miss Ferrars?" Alicia coaxed.

"We'll see what Con can give us before we talk of

producing it," Miss Ferrars said prudently. "What about it, Con?"

"I don't mind trying to write something for that," Con said with equal caution. "I can have a shot at it and show it to you and you'll say if you think it's good enough, but I've never done a real play before, Miss Ferrars."

"Very well, then; that's settled! Remember how many people you have to fit with parts, Con, and I implore you not to ask us for too elaborate dresses! Of course," she added, "you all realise that when it's ready the Sale committee will have to see it and decide if it will do, don't you?"

Several faces told her that they had never given a thought to this. She laughed outright. "Don't look so dropped on! I see no reason why you shouldn't put up a good show if you do your best. Now clear away, or you'll be late for the bell. It's due to ring in two minutes' time."

They exclaimed loudly and there was a rush to get everything cleared up. If they were late when the bell went, Matron would have plenty to say to them. Miss Ferrars came to the rescue and packed everything away as they brought it to her. When the bell finally rang, there was only Len's treadle fretsaw to push into the corner where it lived and the cloth on which she worked to keep the sawdust from messing the floor to gather up and shake outside. Miss Ferrars volunteered to see to that and sent them off in good time.

They might not talk on the stairs or in the corridors; but once they were in their own dormitory, Len turned to Rosamund who slept next door to her and said fervently, "You know, I think we're jolly lucky to have Ferry for our form mistress. I think I'm going to ask her to talk over my idea with me. If she thinks it'll do, I'll send it in and—well, I shall tell our crowd, only you'll have to promise to say nothing to anyone else."

"Then I hope she agrees!" Rosamund cried as she pulled off her frock on the other side of the dividing curtain. "I'm dying to know what it is!"

"You'll know—if they use it!" Len retorted. "And now shut up! I'm going to say my prayers."

CHAPTER SEVEN

MATRON

"THAT you, Joey? Is Jack at home? I want to speak to him."

"Oh, Hilda, *must* you? He's had a hectic three days of it and only got home around four this morning, dead tired and awfully down. That poor little Mrs Milward died last night and you know how he hates to lose a patient. Oh, yes; I know that only a miracle could have saved her and she wasn't sorry to go. She told me so when I visited her last week. All the same, when it happens he will keep on wondering if it would have made a difference if he'd done this or that or tried the other. It never would, of course; but that doesn't keep him from worrying about it. There isn't anything badly wrong with you, is there?—No epidemics?"

"No epidemics; but Matey heard this morning that her sister died last night. They operated on Monday and she never recovered consciousness—thank goodness!" Miss Annersley ended fervently.

"Was it as bad as that? Then I agree. How's Matey? She hasn't collapsed?" There was fear in Joey Maynard's voice as she finished and Miss Annersley promptly relieved it.

"Oh, no; she hasn't actually collapsed, but she's looking very worn. She says that she knew it was coming, but no matter how much you are prepared, it's a shock when it happens. She wants to go on with her work here and I agree that she ought to be at it again soon. She's the kind that can get comfort from work. But just at present, she's very far from fit and I want her to come to you for a few days."

"You know we'll be glad to have her; but isn't she going home?"

"Not at present. Joan and the children are with Mr Harper and honestly, I don't think Matey's fit for the journey. She'll go later on when she's had time to pull up. At present I want her to have a complete rest. The only thing is, she won't listen to me, though I've talked myself nearly hoarse trying to persuade her. That's why I want Jack. He can set a large and heavy foot firmly on her ideas and take her over to Freudesheim—and *you*."

Joey flushed as she replied. "Oh, Hilda, that's one of the nicest things you've ever said to me! I'll go and tell him and he'll come. Pack a nightie and her washing and hair things to be ready for him. You can see to the rest and bring or send it later in the day. I'll fly and see to the bedroom while Jack comes along. He'll soon put an end to any objections! See you later, I suppose. Goodbye!"

Joey banged the receiver down on its cradle and went racing upstairs and along the corridor to the big room where her husband lay sleeping peacefully. She stood looking down at him for a moment, regret in her face. Jack really was very tired. Then she roused him by the simple method of sitting down heavily and suddenly on his legs.

"Wake up, old man! You're pretty badly wanted!"

He rolled over, mumbling, "Whazzat?" Then he roused fully and sat up. "Who wants me? Move off, Joey! You're a ton weight!"

Joey stood up. "Oh, Jack! I'm sorry to have to wake you, but you'll have to go over to the school and talk sense to Matey. I've just had a call from Hilda. Lilian Harper is gone—died last night without regaining consciousness and Matey is pretty well bowled over, Hilda says. She wants us to have her for a few days till she can pull herself together again, but Matey doesn't seem to see it in the same light and won't listen. Go and see what you can do like a dear while I get a room ready for her."

Jack threw back the clothes and scrambled out of bed. "O.K. You run and give Hilda a ring and tell her I'll be along in twenty minutes—I've got to shave, you know—and I'll see to it. She'd better let Matey alone till then. Arguing will only make her dig her toes in harder than ever."

"Right!" Joey vanished, but came back presently, just

as he left the bathroom, bearing a cup of steaming coffee with her. "You haven't had any breakfast, so just wrap yourself round this before you go. I won't bother you with food. Lunch will be ready in an hours' time, anyhow. Just nice time for you to collect Matey and bring her along."

He grinned at her as he took the cup. "Thoughtful woman! Did you get Hilda?"

"No; she was teaching. But I gave Rosalie your message and she said she would see to Matey's belongings and pack the rest this afternoon."

"That's all right, then." Jack finished his coffee and handed the cup back to his wife. "That was good! Went right to the spot! Look, Joey! You go and get that room ready. When I saw Matey last week it struck me she was a good deal under the weather and I should say she'll only be fit for bed. Shove in a couple of bottles. She'll be cold inside, anyhow, and warmth is always comforting. Anyhow, once we get her over here with no more responsibility for anything, she'll probably conk out as you so elegantly express it. So have everything ready, including a bowl of hot soup. Can do?"

"Can do!" Joey went off to obey his behests feeling relieved about him. The prospect of a hard tussle—she knew Matron!—had cleared away the last of Jack's depression. By the time he could think of Mrs Milward again, things would have got into their right perspective once more.

"I'm most awfully sorry about Lilian Harper," she thought as she made up the bed in her best guest-room. "All the same, it's a blessing in disguise where Jack's concerned. And, judging by what Hilda's told me, a blessing for her, too, poor soul! Matey herself will see that presently."

It evidently took Jack some time to battle with Matron's arguments, for lunch had been waiting ten minutes when at last the front door opened and he came in with a supporting arm round Matron's shoulders. Joey was waiting and as they entered, she came forward swiftly and her warm arms were round Matron's little wiry figure.

"Matey, dear! I'm so glad to have you! Come along

71

upstairs to your bedroom and we'll see what a spot of bed will do for you. Don't worry about anything. I'm in charge!"

All the same, she was secretly horrified at the change in Matron. Her fresh colour had faded and her face was pinched and drawn. Her eyes were heavy and she made no response to Joey's loving greeting. She did as she was asked, but quite mechanically, and her hostess was thankful when she was lying in her comfortable bed against the big french pillows, facing the window which looked out towards the Jungfrau—or rather, to where the Jungfrau was. It was a grey day, though no snow had fallen, and the mighty mountain was veiled in mist. Joey made sure that her patient was comfortable and then brought a small bowl of strong, hot soup and fed her as if she had been a baby.

Matron took what was given her in silence. Only, when Joey set the empty bowl aside and bent over her to tuck her in warmly, she caught a faint whisper. "Lilian—is gone."

"Yes," Joey said gently, "and how glad you must be that her sufferings are all over now. She is resting and her poor weary body is at peace."

Her beautiful voice lingered on the last word, but Matron made no response, so the younger woman kissed her again and slipped out and down to the Speisesaal where Jack Maynard had already begun his meal.

"Come along!" he said. "I told the Coadjutor to feed the twins and Cecil in the playroom so that we could talk. Here's your plate. Make a good meal, my dear."

Joey began. When her plate was empty, she looked across the table at him. "Did you have a bad time with her?" she asked.

"Pretty bad. But when she gave in, she did it completely. Hilda's a wise woman, Jo, Gwynneth would have been all in if she'd gone on much longer."

"Gwynneth!" Joey repeated, startled. "Oh, Matey! I'd forgotten that's her name."

"We're going to use it while we're in charge, my dear, so drop the Matey business. The last thing she said to me as she went to put on her cap and coat was, 'Apart from Eric, there's almost no one left to call me Gwynneth now.' I told her there were plenty if she would let us and whether she did or not, you and I were going to set the rest the example. Warn Hilda and Co. when you get a chance."

"All right; but we've all called her "Matey" for so long, it'll be an effort to remember at first. What about diet? I gave her the soup as you said."

"Run her lightly for the next day or two. She'll be all right soon, now we've got her where we want her. But the whole system needs rest. So it'll be best to keep her to soup and milk puddings and so on for the present. Don't worry, Joey. Matey's a fine woman and she'll soon be herself again. Now what about *our* pudding?"

Joey rang the bell and Anna arrived with one of her famous puddings which the doctor ate hungrily. As he said, he had missed his breakfast and needed a solid meal. When it was over, he stood up and stretched.

"Heigh-ho! I must go! I've a few cases to visit and then they want me at San. I'll try to be back for Kaffee und Kuchen, though. I'll just take a dekko at— *Gwynneth* before I go. Then I'll be off. What are you doing with yourself?"

"Work on the new book till Kaffee und Kuchen. Rösli will take the babies for their walk. It's still fine and I like them to be out all they can. Should I leave Matey—I mean Gwynneth—or should I look in on her from time to time?"

"Tell you when I come down."

But when he came down, it was to tell his wife to leave the patient alone. "She's had a weep and is all the better for it. Now she's going to sleep and she'll probably sleep for some hours. I got out of her that she'd had very little this past week. Let her make up for it as much as she can now."

He went after that and Joey, having seen her babies well wrapped up and off for their walk with Rösli, went to the study and put in a good afternoon's work. Jack returned at five—seventeen, by mid-European time—and went upstairs to look at the invalid. She was still asleep and looked very white and wan, but the pinched look was leaving her face, so he felt satisfied.

"How is she?" Joey asked anxiously when he came into the study where she was sitting. "I didn't go near as you said not."

"What I hoped for," he replied, stretching himself on the big settee. "She's sleeping peacefully and looks better already. She's been living under a nasty strain for the past week or so and hadn't slept much. Now she's well away. Don't disturb her for anything. Let her sleep till she wakes of herself."

"Did you give her anything?" his wife demanded.

"To make her sleep? Not a thing! I rather thought that if we could get her to have a good cry, once she was here with no further need to keep up, this would happen."

"Good! Well, I'll write to Joan Alston tomorrow, shall I? And let her know how things are with her aunt. She can tell her father and then they won't expect to hear anything for the next few days. Hilda says in a week or two, if Matey—I mean Gwynneth, I simply can't get used to it!—is well enough, she'll send her home for a week or two later on. There's something weird about that sentence," she added in parenthesis, "but as long as you understand, it's all right."

As it turned out, Matron had nearly a week in bed. At first she slept most of the time. When the Friday came, however, she was much better and taking an interest in things. She asked for the twins and baby Cecil and even, when they were alone together on the Sunday, spoke of her loss to Joey. She said little for she was a deeply reserved woman, but what she did say, told her hostess a good deal.

"Well, you'll still have Mr Harper and Joan and Kenneth," Joey said. "And there are Joan's youngsters—two, isn't it?"

"Yes; I've a lot to be thankful for. I don't need you to tell me that, Jo. But I'm going to miss Lilian terribly. We were chums as well as sisters. All the same," she added firmly, "I'm thankful it's over. She suffered badly these last few months. I can be glad her torment is over."

She insisted on getting up next day and on the Tuesday, she went back to school.

"I'm much better, thanks to you two," she told Joey and Jack before she left. "I needed that rest; but now I'll be better working. Thank you both for all you've done. I can stand on my feet again, thanks to you."

The two Heads were together when she arrived at the school and both reproached her for not taking a longer rest; but she shook her head.

"I won't say I'm sorry for having had these few days of quiet. I can see that they've probably saved me from an illness for I *was* at the end of my tether when Jack Maynard marched me off. But I'm all right now and I'd rather get back to work." Then she asked sharply, "What do the girls know?"

"Nothing!" Miss Annersley said promptly. "We told them you were poorly and Jack had taken you to Freudesheim for peace and quiet."

"Thank goodness for that! Don't tell them any more. There's no need and it's nothing to do with the school. You don't talk about it, either. Words won't help, you know. So far as Lilian herself is concerned, I'm glad. Eric has Joan and her children so he won't be too lonely. And I have my work—and all of you. I'd rather not discuss it."

"I'll tell the others," Miss Annersley said. "As you say, it's no one's business but yours."

So Matron returned and took up her work again and no more was said. In any case, the school was all agog with anticipation of next term's events and, at the moment especially with the ideas they themselves had been asked to suggest. Only Mary-Lou, with her usual keen insight, guessed that more had been wrong than they had been told and she kept her thoughts strictly to herself until she could see Joey and ask her about it.

Meanwhile, the staff gave Matron a rapturous welcome and after Abendessen that evening, the school was handed over to the care of the prefects and every mistress in the place scurried off to the staff sitting-room which had been appointed as the place for the coming debate. The younger mistresses pushed tables together to make one long one, while their seniors devoted themselves to brewing coffee and producing cakes, biscuits and sweets "to lighten labour", as Miss o'Ryan remarked pensively while she nibbled a salted almond.

Miss Wilson arrived with her own mistresses and when coffee had been dispensed by Mlle de Lachennais, the doyenne of the staff room, Rosalie Dene and Gillian Culver, the two secretaries, produced the locked and slotted box into which the suggestions had been dropped.

"Not so many as I dreaded," Miss Wilson commented as Rosalie unlocked the box and tipped out a little pile of folded slips. "I thought we'd be snowed under."

"Oh, that was the prefects," Miss Wilmot, maths mistress, and an Old Girl herself, replied. "I understand they sent round to the form prefects an order that all slips were to be collected and voted on in form and the three that got most votes were to be put into the box and the rest disposed of."

"Whose bright idea was that?" asked Miss Nalder from St Mildred's.

"I gather it came from Mary-Lou and the Gang; but Elinor and the rest leaped at it."

"Good! It saves us a lot of bother," Miss Denny, who taught Italian and Spanish and helped with the junior music, said cheerfully. "How are we doing it?"

"I'll read them out and you can mark them. Five for very good; four for good; three for fairly good. We needn't consider anything under that," Miss Wilson said. "Hand those slips over, Nancy, and the rest of you find your pencils and paper and be quick about it!"

"It's done!" Miss Ferrars said, waving her pencil gaily. "We all came provided. You can go right ahead."

"*Don't* use Americanisms!" was all Miss Wilson vouchsafed as she opened the first slip at which she gazed before giving a chuckle. "A junior, for a ducat! Writing *and* contents give it away."

"What *are* the contents?" Miss Culver demanded.

" 'Have a huge birthday cake, big enough for every one to have a slice and have it at Kaffee und Kuchen on the Sunday of the weekend.' "

76

"And very sensible, too. You always have a birthday cake on a birthday," Miss Denny said. "I'll give that one the full five. It's something we can easily do——"

"Not with *one* cake. No one has a cake-tin big enough," Miss Annersley reminded her gently. "We'll have to have a dozen or more. Still, so far as I'm concerned, they may have their cake."

"And Matey can lay in an extra stock of castor oil for the occasion," added Miss Andrews with a twinkle in her very blue eyes.

"I always have plenty for all requirements," Matron said firmly.

"Well, what's the verdict from the rest of you?" Miss Wilson demanded. "What, full marks from everyone? Shame on you for a greedy crew!"

"Mark it with a five, Nell, and then pass it on to me," Miss Annersley interposed, laughing. "Find me some clips, Rosalie, and I'll bundle them together as the voting goes. Then we'll know where we are at the end."

Rosalie Dene produced a handful of paper-clips and Miss Wilson read the next. " 'Have a very good photographer on the Saturday and have one huge photo of everyone taken. Make a list as we are posed and have it printed on the photo.' "

"What an excellent idea!" Nancy Wilmot exclaimed. "Oh, five for that, everyone! It's really worth it!"

Everyone agreed and Rosalie Dene made a note on her pad to find out about photographers the next time she was in Berne.

"*Here's* a brilliant idea!" Miss Wilson said, sarcasm edging her tones. " 'Build a small chalet and furnish it so that Old Girls can come and stay and visit the school.' Someone isn't in the least practical. She doesn't give any idea as to who is to pay for the chalet and its upkeep. Does she think we're all millionaires by any chance?"

"Down the drain with it!" Miss Burnett exclaimed. "There are plenty of places around where people can stay if they want to come and see us. I call that a most unnecessary expense!"

It was tossed aside and so was the next which proposed

a radical change in the school uniform so that it might be "really artistic".

"What utter rot!" cried the downright Nancy. "There's nothing *in*artistic about our uniform. I call it quite charming, myself, with its fitting top and flared skirt and the colours are beautiful and suit most folk. Who was the idiot who thought out that one?"

"Our priceless Yseult, I expect," Miss Moore said impatiently. "She goes all out for the picturesque. Remember the fuss about that mop of hers last term? Drown it, Nell! We don't want any change. As Nancy says, our uniform's O.K."

"Your slang!" responded Miss Wilson in pained tones. But she crumpled up the slip and tossed it into the nearby waste-paper basket someone had had the forethought to bring in.

The next eight or nine were treated in the same way. They were either so dull that no one wanted them or so wildly expensive, like Norah Fitzgerald's suggestion that the school should have riding classes with its own ponies for the girls, that no one would consider them for a moment.

"And anyway," Miss Annersley remarked, "where does Norah think riding could take place in a mountainous area like this. You don't want ponies up here; you want mules! Really, that child is horses-mad!"

"She always was," her form mistress, Miss Moore, assented. "She means to run a riding school herself when she's grown-up."

"It's the thing she's best fitted for," Biddy o'Ryan said.

"You stop chattering and let me go on with this!" Miss Wilson ordered. "Ah! Here's something good after all that rubbish!" She read out, " 'Make a series of albums with pastel paper interleaved with lined paper. Ask everyone for her photo and any interesting details of her career and number them according to the year each girl came to the school.' How's that everyone?"

"Oh, an excellent idea!" Miss Annersley exclaimed. "I've often wondered about quite a number of the Old

Girls who have lost touch with us. If we had a series of albums that would be a great help and of great interest. A most well thought-out idea. Whose is it, Nell? Do you know!"

"Someone from St Mildred's—but I'm giving no secrets away!" Miss Wilson retorted as she handed the slip over and took up the next which was also the last.

Once more her face lit up and she looked round the rest. "This is the best of them all and a real way of commemorating our coming of age! I wonder who thought of it?"

"What *is* it?" Peggy Burnett demanded frantically. "You might read it to us, Bill, and not sit there nattering over it!"

"Are you addressing *me*?" Miss Wilson demanded majestically.

"I am. What's more, I'm not apologising, either. You're being aggravating on purpose!" retorted Peggy, twinkling at her Head Mistress who gave it up and laughed.

"Bright girl! However, to be serious, I do really think this is the best idea of the lot and I'd like to know who thought of it. I don't know the script at all."

"Oh, if it's script, it might be anyone's," Miss Derwent pointed out. "Read it to us and let's see if we think the same."

Miss Wilson complied. " 'Ask every one for a subscription to begin to build our school chapels.' "

The staff received it in momentary silence. Then Biddy o'Ryan exclaimed, "Oh, good! I'll give a tenth of next term's salary to that if you think we can do it. We need those chapels very badly and a better way of celebrating I can't think of!"

"I'll do the same!" Nancy Wilmot chimed in. "I think it's a marvellous idea!"

Mlle de Lachennais nodded. "Moi aussi! I have now no one but myself to consider and I can do it quite well. And you Julie?" She smiled at her confrère Mlle Berné, whose work lay mostly with the St Mildred people.

"I agree," Julie Berné replied. "To have our own

chapels would be a blessing. We have much need of them."

"Well," Miss Moore said, "as you all know, I'm helping my brother to educate his two boys so I can't rise to such heights; but I'll give all I can."

Matron, seated at the end of the table, looked up. "If we can do it, I should like to give a window in memory of my sister."

"And I," said Miss Annersley, "will give one in memory of those girls who have been called to Higher Service during the years."

There was no doubt about it. Everyone felt that this, of all ways, was the best to celebrate the coming big event. Every one of the mistresses eagerly promised a subscription and the two Heads knew that former members of the staff would be delighted to join in. Finally, Miss Annersley called for silence and when she got it, wound up the talk.

"I quite agree that this will be the best way of all to mark the year. We must consult Madge Russell, of course, but I know she will agree. Say nothing to anyone about it yet, for we can't decide such a big thing until we have heard from her. The rest of the ideas may be typed out, Rosalie, and put on the notice board in Hall for the girls to consider. I think you'd better add that there is one other idea which we are very much hoping to use but it is too big a thing to tell them yet as we must consult other people first. All the rest can be done by the school. I doubt if we can manage everything, but the girls must vote in any case."

Blushing wildly, Kathie Ferrars got to her feet. "May I speak, please? There's just one thing I'd like to tell you all. I know we said all suggestions must be anonymous, but I'm going to break that over this last suggestion. It was begun by Len Maynard and worked out to its present form by the other two, Rosamund Lilley, Betty Landon, Jo Scott, Emerence Hope and Alicia Leonard. They brought it to me to vet and I told them to leave it with me. I put it into the box myself, so no one but that crowd knows anything about it. I felt as Miss Annersley says—

that it's too big a thing for girls to discuss until Lady Russell and Mrs Maynard and people like that have seen it." Then she sat down.

Rosalie Dene looked round them. "May I make a suggestion, please? It is that we make a list of all subscriptions promised tonight and send that to Madame so that she will know that we all support the fund with all our hearts. It would help her to decide just how possible it would be to do it."

"I agree," Miss Wilson said promptly. "Make a list of our names, Rosalie, and pass it round and we'll all scribble down what we're prepared to give. Then you can type it out and we'll send it off to Wales at once. The sooner this is decided, the better."

Rosalie set to work and as the mistresses left the room at the end of the meeting, each came to her and added the amount she was prepared to subscribe towards the cost of building and equipping the two private chapels.

Matron was the first for she was tired now and wanted to go to bed. She had been rather dreading this first night in her old room after the shock of her sister's death, but once she was in bed, she was so occupied in considering what her window should represent, that she was asleep before she knew it and when the morning came, she was refreshed and ready for the work that, as she had truly said, would prove her greatest comfort.

CHAPTER EIGHT

INTER V CREATE A SENSATION

MISS DENE woke early next morning, so she got up, dressed, and ran down to the office to type out the final list of ideas accepted by the staff for next term and then pinned it up on the notice board in Hall with a virtuous feeling that she had kept no one waiting this time.

Nina Rutherford, the school's musical genius, was allowed to practise on the grand piano in Hall, which was something with which Rosalie had forgotten to reckon. Her own intention had been to put up the list so that when the girls arrived for prayers, they would have time to read it and a minute or two for discussion before work started for the day. But Nina, entering Hall for her usual half-hour of scales and exercises before Frühstück, caught sight of the fresh sheet against the green baize, forgot all about music for once, and made a beeline to the board where she stood entranced for nearly five minutes. In fact, it was only when she heard Miss Lawrence, head of the music, speaking to someone outside, that she remembered what she ought to be doing and fled to the piano to pitch in at her Tausig modulatory exercises with a vim!

This was something new for Nina, who was usually inclined, as most genius is, to be single-minded. At the beginning of her school career, a year ago now, nothing could have come between her and her piano; but the year spent at the Chalet School had helped to modify this slightly. Music would always be the be-all and end-all of her life; but her interests had certainly widened.

Once she was at the piano, however, next term's doing faded from her mind and she gave all her attention to what she was doing, listening to her finger-work with a concentration that Miss Lawrence and her coadjutors were wont to wish their own pupils would imitate. However, when the bell rang for Frühstück and the end of the half-hour, she suddenly remembered.

"I say!" she exclaimed, speaking in English which was the official language for the day, "the list of suggestions for next term is up on the board in Hall!"

Virginia Adams, seated three beyond her, leaned across the others to ask eagerly. "Can you remember any of them, Nina? What are they?"

"A thoroughly mixed grill," Nina replied with a grin. She attacked her porridge and devoured three spoonfuls before she obligingly relieved the wild curiosity her remark had roused in everyone. "One is to have a huge birthday cake on the day. It's to be big enough for everyone to have a slice."

"That's a junior!" Barbara said with conviction. "It sounds like our young Janice—or Ailie Russell or Judith Willoughby or some of that crowd."

"It might equally well be a junior middle. They're all tummy at their age," Josette Russell said, spooning up porridge at a great rate. "*That* wasn't all, surely? Go on, Nina! What else?"

"Well, some bright spark has proposed having a huge photo of everyone present on the principal day. I'd like that, myself. I wouldn't know the Old Girls, of course, but we could write down the names of those we do know on the back and have it to look back on in the future. I can just see myself, an aged and decrepit dame, showing it to someone and quavering. 'That's Bab Chester. Ah, she was a demon in those days and now she's the grandmother of thirty and completely gaga——' "

"Not with any truth!" Barbara retorted swiftly. "I've no intention of marrying, so the grandchildren simply won't be there! And as for gaga—gaga yourself!"

The rest chuckled at her indignation and then Virginia asked, "Well? What else? Go on, Nina, and do stop being so aggravating!"

"My dear girl, I go to Hall to practise," Nina replied sweetly.

"Don't tell me you didn't read the thing right through, once you'd cocked an eye at it!" her cousin Anthea put in. "You may be a genius, but you're human!"

"Oh, talk sense!" Nina said crossly. Any reference to her great gift made her hot and embarrassed and distinctly annoyed. "Go and look for yourself if you want to know as much as all that!"

"Pipe down, idiot!" Prunella Davidson told Anthea who was her next-door neighbour. "Go on, Nina!"

"Well, there's another photographic suggestion that rather took my fancy."

"What was that?" Verity Carey asked in her silvery voice.

"Well, every single person who's been at the school is to be asked to send a photo and details of her career and they are to be made up into albums and kept—in the library,

I imagine. But what struck me most was the fact that there is an even more important idea to be discussed later on."

Virginia sat back, looking most disappointed. Judging by what Nina said, her own proposal was not there; and yet she had thought it an excellent one. A school as big as the Chalet School *ought* to run a naturalist club. The rest, however, more than made up for the lack of interest she showed. And not only the people at her own table. Some of Nina's remarks had been overheard by the girls sitting at the nearest tables and before the meal was over, most people knew almost as much as she had told. The mistresses sitting in state at the top of the room, caught scraps of chatter, looked at each other and laughed.

"Oh, goodness! I forgot Nina's practice!" Miss Dene exclaimed. "Someone will have to fly to Hall as soon as the meal's over and lock the doors or we shall have them all pouring in to investigate! I'm so sorry, Miss Annersley."

Miss Annersley laughed. "To judge by what I can overhear, Nina must have cut part of her practice for once. Go and lock the doors now, my child, and bring the keys back here to me. That ought to hold the little dears!"

Miss Annersley let the excited chatter go on until the end of the meal. When she rose for grace, she said blandly, "It is a beautiful day, so you will all go for your morning walk. Finish your dormitory work as quickly as you can and put on your nailed boots when you get ready. If the weather holds, you shall have winter sports this afternoon, but we can't let you take the morning off again, I'm afraid, so you must have your walk. Be ready for your escorts, please. No one will be excused this morning."

"I should think not!" Miss Derwent remarked. "We're well into February now and everyone is prophesying an early spring so we may expect rain before long, I suppose. That will mean few walks. When it rains here, it *rains*! They'll be weatherbound all right in two or three weeks' time! We must make the most of our opportunities to get them out while this sunshine lasts."

The staff laughed again, causing Elinor Pennell to observe to Sybil Russell who sat next to her that the staff seemed to be enjoying themselves this morning. When the news got round that the doors of Hall had been locked against them, the prefects disgustedly declared that this was what had amused them.

"It amazes me that Nina should have forgotten her dear music long enough to read the list," Mlle remarked when she met two or three of the others in the staff room after the school had departed, grumbling hard at having to wait.

"Oh, Nina comes to earth a little oftener than she used to," responded Miss Armitage who was that young lady's form mistress. "They're all getting very excited about next term. I only hope it won't affect the exam results!"

"Not it!" said Biddy o'Ryan cheerfully. "Anyhow, aren't they going to go all out to make a record term of it next term? 'Twas Mary-Lou was talking about it the other day. They'll work all right, so don't worry, me dear."

"I only hope you're right," Miss Armitage murmured.

"Sure, an' I know I am," Biddy returned as she sorted out history essays. "They're doing better already. I'll have to be hoisting up me standard for essays if they go on at this rate. I've seven A plusses in Va and four in Inter V."

Among the girls, one of the most annoyed because the doors of Hall were locked against them had been Yseult Pertwee. As Miss Moore had shrewdly guessed, it was she who had suggested altering the school uniform. She was very anxious to see if it would be accepted and now she must wait! The idea had been passed by the form only because no one else seemed to have very much to propose, Len having consulted Miss Ferrars about hers and been told to say nothing about it to anyone. Yseult even ventured to try to peep in at the window as they lined up outside Hall, but the board was between two of the windows, so she had her pains for nothing.

When they came back from the walk, glowing with brisk exercise in the chilly air, they had to fly to their form rooms as soon as they had changed to get out everything they needed for the first lesson. But that done, Len Maynard led the way to Hall and the doors were unlocked, Rosalie Dene having done it once they were well away. They streamed in and rushed over to the notice board which they scanned eagerly. Nor were they the only ones. Representatives from most forms followed them in and there was a perfect mob milling round that particular spot in Hall. Yseult, taller than most of her form, looked eagerly across the heads of the rest and gave vent to an exclamation of vexation.

"What's wrong with *you*?" Joan Baker demanded.

"Oh!" she cried in choked tones. "We've still got to wear this dull, stupid uniform! It's *too* much!"

"I told you it wouldn't have a chance of being considered," said Margot Maynard with more truth than tact. "I thought it mad myself."

"Did you really expect we'd change when it's only three years or so since we changed before?" Heather Clayton demanded.

"Besides, I don't want to change, anyhow," put in Francie Wilford. "I think our blue and silver and crimson are awfully pretty. And next term when we wear our cottons, we can have any colour we like so long as it's the same pattern."

"Tunics are the ugliest and most unbecoming dress there is!" Yseult retorted. "You can't make them pretty, whatever you do. And skirts and blouses are no better."

"Oh, raspberries to that!" Emerence Hope interjected. "What *you* mean is that they aren't picturesque—whatever that may be! We look trim and workmanlike and that's what we want in school. You don't want to go round looking like—like the Lady of Shalott in a fit! And those dripping sort of sleeves and miles of skirts'ud be a perfect pest! I know where mine would be most of the time— into everything they oughtn't and *wouldn't* Matey have something to say!"

"Don't worry," said Jo with her usual blunt common sense "No one in their senses would ever agree to schoolgirls being dressed like that—*or* having their hair all over the place!"

"Besides," Rosamund Lilley added her quota, "our people would be awfully annoyed if they had to buy us all new things at once."

"Oh, you're all too childish to understand!" Yseult exclaimed. "It's waste of time trying to make any of you see sense! You've no idea of beauty!" and she flung off, thoroughly disgruntled.

"That's a good idea—about the birthday cake, I mean," Charmian Spence murmured. "But I suppose our Yseult is much too grown-up to be interested in anything so common as *eats*!"

Barbara Chester was reading the list. "I like the albums idea the best of the lot," she announced. "There'll be quite a little bit to put in for Beth."

"Your sister that got married last June, you mean?" Prunella asked.

Barbara nodded. "She's done quite a few things and now," her eyes gleamed with satisfaction, "she's going to have a baby in August. I'll be an aunt then. And so," she added with a peal of laughter, "will that kid Janice!"

The first bell rang at that point and they all had to go. But not before the final statement had roused their curiosity to the deepest pitch. Con Maynard had complained that she couldn't read through people's heads and big Joan Baker had obliged by reading it aloud for everyone.

" 'There is one more suggestion, but it is too big a thing to be decided until Lady Russell and the other members of the Board of Governors have been consulted. It will be announced when their decision is given.' "

"Wonder what it is?" Betty Landon said as Inter V moved off in a body.

Two or three people eyed each other doubtfully. Could it be the idea Len had propounded to them and which they had all discussed so eagerly with Miss Ferrars the other evening? Emerence was sure of it and so was Margot. The rest were inclined to be dubious. In any case, they could say nothing there and the bell had rung. They had to scramble to their seats and were there just in time before the door opened and their form mistress arrived to take register.

After prayers, Miss Annersley told them that all the ideas on the list would be adopted. The birthday cake—cakes, rather—would be made and decorated by the seniors in cookery class. Both photographic suggestions were commended and the various details connected with the albums were given to the girls. Miss Dene would arrange for a good photographer to be at the Görnetz Platz on the Sunday of the important weekend.

"And now I want to speak about the note at the end of the list," she wound up. "It is a very big suggestion indeed, one which would celebrate our coming of age in a really appropriate manner. But it is so big, that we must get permission from the Governors before we can even tell you girls what it is. I am hoping that they will agree. If they do, I know that you will all be delighted with it. I may say that all we mistresses like it best of all. However, that is all I can tell you now. At the moment, that is all. If the weather holds, we are having sports as soon as the rest period is over and will stay out until half-past fifteen. Leave everything ready by your peg before Mittagessen, please. School—stand! Thank you, Miss Lawrence."

Miss Lawrence struck up one of the lively marches they all enjoyed and they marched out to a morning of hard work. They were all wildly excited by this time, but they knew all too well what would happen to anyone who misbehaved, so no mistress had to complain of them more than usual and the early part of the afternoon was spent in a glorious session of ski-ing or coasting until the long shadows falling across the snow warned them that it was time to return to school.

When they finally assembled in their form rooms for the last lesson, it was dusk and all the lights were on. Several of the forms had preparation, but Inter V would normally have had an hour's plain sewing with Mlle de Lachennais in charge. Most of them regarded the hour with resignation. Two or three enjoyed it. The remainder frankly loathed it. Among these last was Charmian Spence who had arrived at the school the previous term with a well-deserved reputation for ill-doings. This afternoon, what with the morning's excitement and the afternoon's fun, Charmian was ripe for anything. As she sat down with the underslip she was making, she looked round discontentedly. Who would be expected to sit there, hemming round the bottom of a slip when they were feeling all revved up inside? A sudden idea struck her and a cherubic smile overspread her face.

Not that she did anything immediately. Miss Charmian was too canny for that. She set to work meekly on the fine stitchery Mlle demanded, sewing carefully. Presently, Mlle herself arrived to see what she was doing. She commended the sewing but exclaimed in horror at the very dirty hands. Charmian, who had stooped down to rub them over the floor, said nothing, though inwardly she was chuckling to herself.

"But Charmian! What hands!" Mlle exclaimed in her fluent English with its pretty accent. "Put down your needlework and go and wash, I beg you! And never—but *never*!—come to this class with such dirty hands again!"

"I'm sorry, Mlle," Charmian said in her humblest tones.

"Then make haste! This lesson is a half-hour short, and you must not waste time."

Charmian laid the slip neatly on top of her desk and scudded off to the splashery where she held her hands under the tap and then wiped them off with the towel, leaving ample proof of the sketchiness of her washing.

In the form room, Mlle continued to make her rounds. Heather Clayton, in difficulties over her buttonholing, got up to take the work to her. At the same moment Margot, also in difficulties, got to *her* feet. And that moment, all the lights went out!

There was an instant turmoil. Margot bounced into Heather and the pair of them collapsed on to the floor where they made the confusion worse by groping about, grabbing the ankles of the nearest people who shrieked promptly and stooped to push them off and were hauled down into the melée. Jo Scott jumped and ran her needle into her finger. Several other people also jumped and sent their workbaskets flying so that reels of cotton, packets of needles, scissors, pins and thimbles showered in every direction. Len Maynard leaping up with the laudable intention of opening the door to let the light from the corridor stream in, trod heavily on Yseult's fingers. She had been dragged down by Heather and was just beginning to lever herself up. The squeal she gave outdid anything that happened previously and she slapped vigorously at Len's foot with her free hand, exclaiming, "Get off my hand—get off my hand! You're crushing the fingers to pieces!"

Len tried to do so. She backed hurriedly and sat down firmly on Heather who was still sprawling. At the same time, one foot flew out and kicked the ill-used Yseult on the shoulder drawing another yell from her, by which time Mlle, cautiously feeling her way along the wall, had contrived to get to the door and fling it open only to show an even blacker darkness there.

She turned round. "Be quiet, mes filles!" she said in her firmest tones. "A fuse has blown, no doubt. Gaudenz will attend to it and we shall have light. Meanwhile, be silent! Remain where you are! Who is it that screams so? Be still! You are none of you babies here, I hope!" This last in her most withering tones.

The free fight which had been taking place in the aisle ceased, and Jo stopped wringing her finger which was bleeding freely for she had driven the needle well in. Those girls who had been taking advantage of the darkness to add to the confusion suddenly came to their senses and tried to get back to their seats before Mlle should find out that they had left them. Only Yseult was sobbing loudly. Len was no light weight and she had come down on the maltreated hand with all her force. Mlle spoke again, even more severely.

"Who is that who weeps? Be silent, I say! There is nothing to fear and—Ah!" she continued in a rather different tone. "Here comes the lights!"

The lights had gone out all over the house. In the kitchen, Karen, who ruled her staff with a rod of iron, had hushed the screaming maids at once before she produced a big electric torch and by its light, rooted out some packets of candles which she sent round by the girls. At the same time Miss Ferrars, who had been in her bedroom, tidying a drawer, also appeared with her torch and in a few minutes there was light of a sort in most places. Two minutes after that, the lights came on again with the same suddenness as they had disappeared. Mlle looked round her disordered class.

Heather and Len were both dirty as to face and blouse. Yseult was even worse. She had lost the ribbon off her plait and her hair had come loose and was tossed all about her, a mantle of golden glory. It was a pity that the rest of her appearance did not match. Between dust from the floor and her tears, she looked a grotesque object, her cheeks streaked and stained and a huge smudge across her chin. Margot's blazer had been buttoned up, so her blouse had escaped the worst, but someone had upset the box of chalk and trampled on it and her hair was powdered white. The floor was scattered with the contents of various work-baskets and quite a number of garments had fallen on the floor, been trodden on and looked as if they had been used for floor-cloths. It was a mercy that, as seniors, Inter V used fountain pens or biros, so there was no ink to spill. But there was quite mess enough. Sitting in her desk, looking as if she had never stirred from it, was Charmian, looking positively seraphic. Len Maynard saw her and her jaw dropped. She needed no one to tell her who had been responsible for all the trouble.

It was unlucky for Charmian that Miss Ferrars, who had been having a few words with Mlle, turned and also saw her. Charmian did *not* see the look of comprehension that lit up the mistress's face. She was too much occupied in looking, as Kathie Ferrars afterwards told her colleagues, "Oh, no, ma'am, *I* ain't seen your canary!" Miss Ferrars murmured a brief sentence to Mlle and then left the room. Mlle's eyes had flashed as she heard what Kathie had to say. But she was an old hand and she kept her head. She told the girls to clear up the mess at once and waited by her table until the room was once more spick and span.

"Charmian!" she said, when they were all sitting down again.

Charmian stood up, looking like the good child from an old-fashioned story book.

"Yes, Mlle?" she said in her most proper voice.

Mlle was not to be taken in. "Tell me," she said slowly, "how did you turn off the lights? Also, I wish to know *why* you did it?"

Charmian's face fell. Whoever would have expected Mlle to be so quickly off the mark? It was an ordinary, naughty little schoolgirl who replied, "I—I turned off the main switch, Mlle."

"I sent you to wash your hands," Mlle said. "The main switch is nowhere near your splashery."

"Oh, I *did* wash them," Charmian protested, spreading out a pair of hands that were certainly clean after a fashion.

Mlle looked at them. "Come here and stand by me, Charmian. I wish to examine your hands more closely."

Charmian came up the aisle very reluctantly, and held out her hands. Mlle lifted first one and then the other and examined them thoroughly. She let them drop.

"And now you will tell me how you reached the main switch. It is kept locked up, too. How did you open the door?"

"Please, Mlle, I saw Gaudenz doing something to the fuse-boxes when we came in and he went away and left the key in the lock. Karen called him. I—I—"

"Eh bien? What did you do?"

Charmian took a long breath. "I—took it out and put it in my pocket," she said.

"Ah! I comprehend!" Mlle stood looking meditatively at the culprit which did not add to Charmian's comfort. In fact, she was nearly ready to yell before the languages mistress finally said, "Well, you have wasted our time and made us all late for Kaffee und Kuchen. There are here," she counted rapidly, "twenty-one of us altogether."

Charmian gazed at her wonderingly and the bell rang for Kaffee und Kuchen. Mlle turned to the rest of the form.

"Leave your work here," she said. "Charmian will put it away for you. Do not go to change. You may change after Kaffee und Kuchen. Tell whoever is on duty that I will come and explain to her myself later. Jo, you will come when your meal is over and tell me who it is."

"Yes, Mlle. I—I think it's Sybil Russell and Blossom Willoughby," Jo stammered.

"Thank you, ma petite. Then I need not trouble you. You will all go and change after your meal and I myself will see Matron and beg her to inform the House matrons. Now you may go."

They went out quietly. Mlle might be a dear and very jolly, but with that look on her face they knew better than to risk rousing her. Mlle waited until Jo Scott went out shutting the door behind her. Then she turned to the sinner who was already repenting the mischief she had done.

"Fold every garment and put it away in its basket and put the baskets neatly into the cupboard," she said briefly as she strolled over to the table and sat down.

Charmian did as she was bidden in a profound silence that told her that *this* time, she really had done it! Mlle waited until it was done. Then she stood up.

"Now," she said, "you may go and get your meal. I have no wish to annoy Karen any further or cause her any more trouble than you have already given her. When you have changed, you will come to me in the staff room and I will take you to Miss Annersley. There, you will tell her what you have done and ask her permission to apologise to the school after prayers. No!" For at this awful fiat, Charmian had begun to babble wildly. "I will hear no more from you. You may go."

Before her stern gaze, Charmian fell silent. She trailed off out of the room repenting even more bitterly the wicked impulse which had made her turn off the electric switch. Oh how she wished she had never laid eyes on Gaudenz that afternoon! It would be bad enough to have to go and confess to the Head. Charmian guessed she was in for a bad time there. But to have to go up to the dais and stand on it and apologise to the entire school seemed too awful to be borne!

Somehow she got through her Kaffee und Kuchen, though every mouthful seemed to choke her. She changed, fighting her tears all the time. She went to Mlle who took her to the study and handed her over to the Head. Miss Annersley had very little to say, but by the time she had finished, what was left of Charmian would have gone into a thimble. Her preparation was of the sketchiest quality that evening and she got into serious trouble next day. But worst of all was standing on the dais, owning up to the entire school, staff, prefects, girls and kitchen staff, for Miss Annersley had insisted that they should be included as they had suffered inconvenience as much as anyone. Finally, when she had humbly begged everyone's pardon, Matron took her shoulder and walked her off to bed. Charmian was thankful to get there. Her pillow was bedewed with tears before she finally fell asleep. But for the rest of the term there was no better behaved girl in the whole school than Charmian Spence!

CHAPTER NINE

THE STAFF CREATE A SENSATION

"IT'S a beast of a day!" Mary-Lou turned from the window in the prefects' room with a disgusted look on her face and came to perch on the table beside Hilary.

"Are you telling me?" Blossom Willoughby demanded. "I loathe this warm wind! It makes you feel sticky and messy and everyone will be on edge and we may look out for trouble with the middles, let me tell you."

"Don't you mean Inter V?" Nan Herbert asked with a giggle.

The rest joined in her giggles. Charmian's exploit of the week before had tickled the fancy of the grandees of the school and, as Sybil Russell had remarked pensively at the time, she had certainly added another to the many stories among the unwritten history of the school. That yet another such yarn was imminent was unknown to them, of course and, in fact, none of them heard of it until their schooldays lay behind them. It belonged to the staff as did another such tale which was beginning to circulate among the people who had been middles six or seven years before, though until now, they had heard nothing of it.

When the prefects were grave again, Hilary Bennet gave her opinion. "If you ask me, Charmian's had such a doing that Inter V will sit heavily and truly on any young hopeful who tries such a mad trick again."

The rest fully agreed with her and then Elinor turned back to the subject of the weather. "I hate the Föhn myself. Quite apart from the fact that it upsets everybody and makes them appallingly irritable, it ruins the snow. Our fun is ended—for the time being, at any rate."

"Yes; but only for the time being. This is still February," Mary-Lou reminded her. "We'll get more frost and snow presently. That's what always happens when the Föhn begins to blow as early as this."

Lesley Malcolm looked up from Rosamund Lilley's autograph album in which she was painting a charming cluster of gentians and other alpine flowers—from memory since all the flowers were still buried deep under the snow. "I don't like it for that reason, but still more because of a much more serious reason—avalanches! You know what happens when the Föhn begins to blow at all steadily. It softens the snow which falls from its own weight and brings down trees and boulders with it and it can cause such awful damage. It isn't likely to affect us hereabouts, of course. We aren't given to bad avalanches here and the pines grow thickly and scatter the wretched things, anyhow. But other places aren't so lucky."

Mary-Lou nodded. "Let's hope it's only a brief effort and we get a good north wind to freeze things up again."

Lesley had turned back to her painting and she continued with a leaf as she said, "That's the best thing that could happen—Ow! Don't shake the table, Bess! You nearly made me splotch my alpine roses with green and a nice mess that would have made of the page!"

"Sorry!" Bess, the art prefect, came round the table to look. "I say! That's a honey! Why on earth don't you take extra art, Lesley?"

"Because I simply haven't the time. I must stick in at my maths. I want to do well in Higher. If I do, when I leave school I'm to go into Dad's office—he's a chartered accountant, you know—and have a shot at the exams. I'd love it if I could do it. Anyhow, it's only flowers I can do at all decently. You've heard Herr Laubach on the subject of my design! And I'm no use at figures or landscape. I only wish I were."

"How *can* you!" exclaimed Mary-Lou, wrinkling her short straight nose disgustedly.

"Good gracious Mary-Lou! What's wrong with wishing that?" Bess cried.

"I didn't mean that, you ass! I rather like painting flowers myself and design can be fun. I was referring to the chartered accountant business."

"Oh, well, Lesley's always been a mathematical genius," Hilary said soothingly.

"And we all know that you are anything but!" Sybil added. "You're about as good as I am and you know what Willy thinks of *my* maths!"

Mary-Lou laughed. "Oh, beneath her notice! So are mine! I'm not going to worry as you don't need, either. You, my lamb, are a genius at needlework and thank goodness, Miss o'Ryan thinks my history isn't too dusty, which is a good thing for me, seeing my future career lies with archaeology. We two can *miss* maths."

Sybil laughed. "And oh, how glad I am I've done with them! I always hated the things. I'm like Aunt Joey there. I believe Mummy was always fairly good."

A dull roar sounded and with one accord the prefects made for the windows and peered out.

"An avalanche—and a whacker to judge by the sound!" Blossom exclaimed. "I wonder whereabout it is? Nowhere near here, of course."

"Probably around the Jungfrau. I believe they get some crashers there," Nan observed.

"I hope it hasn't done any harm," Elinor said anxiously. After three years more or less in the Oberland, they all knew how terribly dangerous a really big avalanche could be. And this was the bad time when the snow was old and most of the oxygen had gone from it.

"Well," Nan stood up and gathered up her books, "we can't do anything about it and it's just on bell-time. Come on, everyone due for extra French. Mlle won't love us if we're late!"

The prefects left it for the time being and moved off, some to go to Mlle, others to a session with Miss Wilmot, the remainder, consisting of Sybil, Nan, Mary-Lou, Hilary and Blossom to join the non-prefects in VIb for one of the Head's delightful lectures in English literature.

Mary-Lou's hope remained unfulfilled. The Föhn blew strongly for the next three days and accounts of bad damage done by avalanches in the eastern part of the country began to come in. Everyone complained of a sticky, gritty feeling and by the Thursday, tempers were very badly on edge. It was the more trying that St Mildred's were hard at work on the final rehearsals for their pantomime. They used Hall for these, and evening after evening the girls, more or less trying to work despite the nervous irritability which affected them all, were not soothed by the peals of laughter that now and then came to them from St Mildred's.

The person worst affected was Nina Rutherford. As a rule, Hall was her practising preserve and when St Mildred's was in possession, she had to find any piano that happened to be vacant. As her standard was very high, as might be expected of a person who was already looking forward to the day when she would emerge as a professional pianist, and the ordinary pianos were what might be expected when some fifty odd girls used them each day, she felt that she had a real grievance. It was unfortunate that, in the wet, messy condition of the snow, no one would hear of her going over to Joey Maynard's where she had a standing invitation to use the magnificent Bechstein in the Salon.

"I wish to goodness this beastly weather would *stop*!" she said crossly to Barbara Chester on the Thursday morning. "I simply can't practise decently on the things most of you people go thumping every day. All my

97

evening practice is being messed up and I've simply *wasted* my time this week!"

"Oh, well, the panto comes off next Wednesday, so it'll only be a few days longer now," Barbara said soothingly. "Why don't you pitch in at your written work and get ahead with that and then take the time next week when Hall is free again?"

"Because it wouldn't be allowed!" Nina snapped back. "I'll have to stick to scales and exercises. I certainly can't do much with anything else!" And she stalked off, her long black pigtail swinging indignantly as she went.

"What on earth's wrong with her?" Barbara demanded of the room in general. "It isn't as if she'd had to stop her practice altogether. She *can* have any spare piano."

"Fed up!" her cousin Anthea said succinctly. "That's what comes of being a genius, my dear. You be thankful you aren't one. It makes you a sickening nuisance to your friends and relatives at times."

Val laughed and then decided that it was time they were over at the geography room where Miss Moore was waiting for them. Nina was excused and had gone to Hall where she was wrestling joyfully with a Scarlatti sonata and had forgotten her troubles for the time being.

The staff were almost as badly affected by the Föhn as the girls were and people found themselves being hauled up for mistakes which normally would have been passed over with either a laugh or an exclamation. Even Frau Mieders lost her traditional calm and when Emerence Hope was found mixing beeswax with methylated spirit instead of turpentine to make furniture polish, she received a rebuke that made her jump, coming from that quarter. Even Miss Annersley was affected though she contrived to keep her usual tranquillity—in public. In private, she tended to snap. Rosalie Dene came in for most of it and was, accordingly, bad-tempered herself with other folk. There were three promising squabbles in the staff room that evening and several people went to bed that night in a very bad mood.

Miss Ferrars, who had been snapped at by three separate people and who had snapped back with a will, woke up on the Friday morning with a feeling that something had changed. The black feeling which had overhung her for the last two days had gone and there was a freshness in the air. She sat up and sniffed delightedly. Then she shivered. The muggy atmosphere had vanished and its place had been taken by a nipping chill which made her fumble for her bedjacket which she pulled over her shoulders before tumbling out, padding across the floor to the light-switch and switching it on.

"Gosh! It's cold!" she exclaimed aloud as she dived for her dressing-gown and huddled it on quickly. "Where are my slippers? This rug's like ice!"

She found her slippers and shuffled her feet into them. Then she went to the window and peered out. It was all dark and she could see nothing. She looked at her watch and gave an exclamation. "Not five o'clock yet! Much too early to go and break the glad news that the Föhn has gone. I know! I'll make myself a cup of tea!"

Her door was softly opened to admit Biddy o'Ryan who looked wild, since she had lost the ribbons that tied the end of her pigtails and her masses of black hair streamed all round her down to her hips.

"I heard you talking to yourself!" she said as she closed the door behind her. "Sure, the Föhn's gone, thank goodness, and we'll be a lot more cheerful today. Was it tea you were mentioning when I came in?"

"It was. Sometimes I wake early so I brought tea and a spirit stove back with me *and* a morning tea set Auntie gave me for Christmas. Can you drink tea without milk? I haven't any, I'm afraid. But I've everything else—including a kettle."

"Don't you be worrying about the milk. I'll see to that," Biddy said with a chuckle. "You carry on and get the kettle boiled and I'll go down to the kitchen. I know where Karen keeps her milk. I won't be a minute!"

But she was—much longer than that!

Miss Ferrars filled her kettle with water from the bathroom and set the little stove going. She produced her pretty, blossomy china and piled some biscuits on a plate. She hunted out the tin of tea and when the kettle boiled, warmed the pot and then made the tea, covering it with a tiny knitted tea cosy. Still Biddy did not return. Kathie looked at her watch. The history mistress had been gone at least ten minutes.

"What on earth's happening to her?" the younger mistress wondered. "She must be hunting up a cow to get that milk!"

She laughed to herself and then went and opened the door softly. The next moment, she had flung it wide and was racing along the corridor, dim with only its guide lights burning, and down the stairs at top speed. A terrific din was rising from the kitchen regions and she meant to know the reason for it at once. Other doors were opening as she ran, and voices from the dormitories added to the noise.

Down the stairs she shot, along the bottom corridor and through the service door which someone—Biddy o'Ryan, presumably—had hooked back to the wall. Then she catapulted into the big main kitchen where Karen, the stalwart cook, clad only in a thick flannel nightdress with her hair in curling-pins, was gripping a sooty-looking object about half her own height in whom Kathie recognised by the long curling hair—Biddy o'Ryan!

All the maids were there in various forms of undress and the usually spotless premises were liberally sprinkled with soot—or was it soot? Kathie did not wait to inquire. She dashed up, snatched at the black-faced object Karen was clutching and cried, "Karen! It's Miss o'Ryan! Do let go of her! And what is all this awful mess?"

"Fräulein o'Ryan!" Karen ejaculated, releasing her prisoner to throw her hands in the air. She peered into the black face. "But it *is* Fräulein o'Ryan! Pardon, mein Fräulein!" And she went off into such a rigmarole of Low German that Kathie was bewildered and even Biddy, who understood it fairly well, clapped her hands to her ears, sending a small cloud of fine black powder flying over everyone at hand.

It was at that moment that Miss Annersley, still contriving to look stately in her flowing dressing-gown with her shining brown hair in a tightly-screwed pigtail, swept

100

into the kitchen, struck the table sharply with one hand and commanded silence in no uncertain tone.

The exclaiming maids stopped short. Karen was checked in mid-stream and Biddy seizing her advantage, fled to the adjoining scullery to see what hot water and kitchen soap would do to remove the black from her face and hands.

"What is the meaning of this disturbance?" Miss Annersley demanded.

Kathie came forward, quaking. "Miss o'Ryan and I were both awake," she said nervously. "I said I'd make tea for us and as I had no milk, Bid—I mean Miss o'Ryan said she would come down and borrow some from the kitchen while I made the tea. She was so long away, I wondered if anything had happened, so I opened my door and heard the noise and came down to see what was happening."

"But—where *is* Miss o'Ryan?" Miss Annersley exclaimed, looking around.

"I'm here," replied a meek voice as Biddy appeared in the doorway of the scullery, soapy water and black dropping from her hands and arms as she dried her face vigorously on the kitchen towel from behind the door.

"My dear girl! What *have* you done to yourself?" the Head cried, looking at her history mistress with lips that twitched in spite of herself.

"Sure, I wouldn't be knowing at all, at all!" Biddy removed the towel which gave evidence of her activities and showed a face smeared and streaked with black. "I only came for some milk. I opened the cupboard where Karen keeps the tins and the first thing I knew a big tin of something fell from the top shelf on to my head. The lid came off and 'twas smothered in black stuff I was. Then Karen came down and grabbed me before I could say anything——"

"Pardon, mein Fräulein," Karen interrupted in her own language. "I thought I had caught a burglar. I, too, was awake. I heard the steps and the key turning in the door so I came down."

"But what *is* the stuff?" Miss Annersley asked, sitting down. The noise upstairs had died away, so evidently the staff had intervened to stop the girls from coming down. Therefore, she could give her mind to an inquiry.

Karen went suddenly red. "Gnädiges Fräulein," she mumbled, "it is but a powder I would try on the stoves to give them a brilliant polish. My cousin told me it was excellent. I ordered the tin and it arrived today and I put it on the top shelf in that cupboard. Perhaps it was too near the edge and when the door was opened, it fell out. I had loosened the lid, ready to mix some for work in the morning."

"Then for pity's sake, Biddy, stop using hot water!" the Head exclaimed. "If it is some sort of blacking, you must use grease, not water! Go and find Matron and she will give you something to remove it. But don't use soap and water!"

Biddy fled, devoutly hoping that the rest of the school had retired to their rooms by this time. She had no wish to add to the many legends the school owned, having already contributed several during her schooldays and one at least only last year. To add another—and *such* another! —was more than she could face with equanimity. However, she was fortunate this time and she reached Matron's room in safety.

Meanwhile, Miss Annersley, having finally got to the bottom of the story, sent everyone back to bed with the remark that as their rest had been so disturbed, they might have an extra half-hour and Frühstück need not be ready before half-past eight. It was still not much more than half-past five, so they would get another hour and a half, at any rate. She handed Kathie a tin of milk observing that she meant to make tea herself and would expect a jugful of milk to be brought to her room when the tin was opened.

"Have you got a tin-opener?" she added. "No? Then look in that drawer. You should find one there. Now go and make your tea and don't forget my milk."

Kathie fled, crimson to the roots of her hair, and it was a very shame-faced mistress who presently arrived in the

Head's wing where Mlle and Miss Dene had slumbered placidly throughout the affair, with the milk.

"My dear girl, don't look so conscience-stricken!" the Head said laughing. "If anyone is to blame, it's Biddy for prancing off like that to 'borrow' a tin of milk and even more Karen for disobeying my orders and trying out fancy polishes after I told her to stick to the old tried ones. But she *will* do it! She has a craze for samples of the latest thing and this is what happens! In any case, she should have seen to it that that tin was well out of harm's way. Go along and enjoy your tea now. I'm sure you've earned it. Biddy will be along presently, I expect." She paused a moment. Then her eyes danced as she added. "I looked into Matron's room on the way here and *she was treating Biddy's hair with the vacuum cleaner*! I don't suppose any harm's been done and, thank goodness, the girls don't know the cause of the uproar and shan't know, if I've any say in the matter."

"Won't some of our own crowd know?" Kathie asked with a chuckle.

"I didn't see any of them in the kitchen and if they do, we'll keep it to ourselves. It won't be the first time!" Miss Annersley chuckled, too. "You ask Mlle what happened the night Tom Gay thought *she* was catching burglars! But I'll put a stop to any talk. Tell the others I want to see them before Frühstück, will you? Now run along or your tea won't be drinkable!" She went into her room with the milk and Kathie went softly back to her own room where she found the tea stone cold and had to heat it up again. By the time it was ready, however, Biddy had arrived, very clean and with her hair tightly plaited back and secured with Matron's own patent ties warranted not to come off, however wildly you might toss about.

She was in a fine state of giggles, for she had had time to recover from the shock and see the funny side of it all. Kathie told her what the Head had said while they sipped their tea and ate biscuits and Biddy heaved an exaggerated sigh of relief.

"Thank goodness for that! I'd never hear the end of it

if it leaked out! Whatever you do, don't let Joey know! She's the world's worst tease—always was!" She drained the last of her cup and set it down. "I needed that! Are you going back to bed or what are you going to do?"

"I'm going back to bed," Kathie said firmly as she collected the crockery and put it back into her cupboard to wait till later. "Even now, we've a good hour longer before the bell rings and I'm cold. I've refilled your bottle and my own while I was waiting for the tea to heat up again. The bathwater's boiling so we've two nice warm beds to get into and I'd advise you to follow my example and have a cosy nap. Anyhow, the Föhn's gone, thank goodness! It's too dark still to see out, but I'm certain it's snowing again—and freezing too, probably."

Biddy laughed. "Not snowing, me dear! I opened my window before I first came in to you and sorra a flake was to be seen. But the air nearly took the skin off my face! 'Tis a hard frost it is, and thank goodness for that!"

Kathie pulled off her dressing-gown and slippers, rolled into bed and snuggled down. "Thank goodness!" she repeated drowsily. "Switch off the light as you go, will you? I'm sl—eep—y!"

CHAPTER TEN

NINA SAVES THE DAY

THANKS to the change in the weather, everyone in the school brightened up and by the time the day came round for the St Mildred's pantomime, everyone was seething with pleasurable excitement. Those folk who had been chosen to join the chorus and the ballet were excused lessons for the morning. The orchestra was also excused for they were to have a final run-through of the overture which had not gone well enough to please Mr Denny, singing-master at the school and conductor on all such occasions. This included Nina Rutherford who was at the piano and nine other people from the school proper. St Mildred's having decided to keep the speaking parts to themselves this year, could spare only three girls for the orchestra—a flute, a cello and a viola.

"I hope Plato is all right," Meg Whyte, leader of the second violins, said anxiously at Frühstück that morning. "Besides being in a ghastly temper, he had a nasty cough last night—which may have been the cause of the temper."

"Oh, heavens!" cried Mary-Lou who was at the same table. "Don't hint at anything so awful, Meg! Who on earth would conduct if he conked out?"

"No idea—Nina, I suppose."

"Nina? Do you think she possibly could?" Hilda Jukes demanded.

"She's conducted for rehearsals," Vi Lucy, who was leader of the orchestra replied. "Oh, I know it's one thing to conduct when it's only us there and another before an audience; but after all, she's going to be a professional pianist, isn't she? She'll have to get accustomed to that sort of thing."

"And if Plato's out of it, can you tell me who else there is?" Meg chimed in.

"What about Lawrie?" Mary-Lou suggested. "She runs most of the music here."

"Lawrie couldn't possibly take over at a moment's notice like that. She hasn't had a thing to do with it," put in Madge Watson. As Madge was music prefect, she was listened to with due respect as one who *must know*.

Meanwhile, sharp eyes at Inter V table had noticed already that both Miss Denny and Matron were absent from the staff table. Sharper wits were quick to draw the inference, especially when they belonged to Emerence Hope and the three Maynards who were all singers and all in the chorus, while Eve Hurrell and Francie Wilford were in the ballet as Chinese frogs with a very funny dance.

"Sally-go-round-the-moon isn't at Frühstück!" Len exclaimed during a pause. "Plato was coughing his head off at our practice yesterday. I do hope he isn't ill!"

"I thought he looked fairly rotten myself," Emerence agreed. "He has to be awfuly careful with colds, hasn't he, Len?"

Len, spooning up porridge, nodded. "Yes. Mamma told me once that ages ago, when the school was in Tirol and he first came to teach at it, they were afraid for him. He's all right as long as he lives in the mountains, but he can't carry on anywhere else. Even here, poor old Sally has fits when he starts a cold."

Rosamund voiced the awful thought that was in all their minds. "Supposing he *is* ill and can't come this afternoon! What on earth will happen then?"

"I wouldn't know," Len replied promptly. "Nina would have to take over, I suppose."

"Nina Rutherford?" Yseult exclaimed, raising her voice incautiously. "Don't talk rot, Len Maynard! She couldn't possibly do it—not if this pantomime is the marvellous affair you all make out. It'll have to be one of the other music people."

"Don't see how it could," Jo Scott said with her usual blunt common sense. "They haven't had the least tip of a finger in the pie. And, so far as that goes, Nina has conducted at some of the rehearsals. *And* she's been accompanist. She does know what's wanted."

Yseult yawned elaborately. "Oh, well, I don't suppose it will really matter. It's only a schoolgirls' show. People won't expect much."

Con Maynard flared up at this. "Oh, won't they indeed? If *that's* what you think, that's where your toes turn in! For one thing, the St Mildred's people are hardly schoolgirls—they're mostly eighteen and nineteen. In case you didn't know," with killing sarcasm, "St Mildred's is the *finishing* branch. Their pantos are always jolly good and people up here know it and expect a lot." She glanced across at the Va table where Nina was busy with rolls and marmalade. "I can tell you, I wouldn't be Nina, if Plato's really ill, for all the tea in China!"

"Neither would I!" Betty agreed. "Fancy having to

106

stand up in the rostrum and conduct in full view of every one! I'd die of fright! Rolls, please, someone!"

Yseult smiled in a superior way as she said, "But then you are hardly musical, are you, my dear Betty? I imagine *your* ideas of conducting would be very odd!"

"I'm as musical as you are!" Betty retorted, flushing angrily. She and Yseult were always at daggers drawn and with her quick temper she was at a disadvantage.

"Oh, I doubt it," Yseult replied blandly. "However, the question doesn't arise."

Alicia, who was great chums with Betty, looked across the table. "Anyhow, if you really *are* better at music than Betty—and I don't see how you can know that seeing neither of you has heard the other—it's the *only* thing you beat her in. She can make rings round you when it comes to everything else and you're more than a year older."

It was about the nastiest thing she could have said. It was Yseult's turn to flush and there might have been wigs on the green, to quote Jo later, but at that point, the prefects on duty came round to see if any more coffee was wanted and the acrimonious discussion ceased. Jo, once Amy Dunne had left their table, changed the subject of conversation on to the ski-ing match which was to take place on Saturday between the House champions and both Yseult and Betty cooled down.

By the time Frühstück ended, however, the entire school was feeling uneasy. Matron arrived before then, it is true, but Mr Denny never showed up.

"You mark my words," Len said as she made her bed at lightning speed. "Plato's gone down with pneumonia or bronchitis or pleurisy or something and Nina will have to conduct this afternoon!"

At prayers, Miss Annersley confirmed their fear. Mr Denny was down with a touch of pneumonia. His sister, Miss Denny, had rung up early that morning from the little chalet down the road from Freudesheim where she and her brother made their home, and Matron had gone at once to see what she could do to help. The doctor had been summoned at six that morning and was returning later. Mr Denny was a delicate man and there was every reason to dread such an illness for him. There could, of course, be no question of his conducting that afternoon.

"Nina Rutherford as deputy conductor will take over," the Head said with a smile at the stunned Nina. "All girls in the orchestra will go straight to St Luke's Hall after they have finished their dormitory work. Miss Lawrence will take you and you may ski there. The only thing we ask is that you will avoid falls. We don't want any damaged players or instruments! Leave your instruments there when you come back. Mittagessen will be at twelve sharp and as soon as it is over, the school buses will be waiting for you so you must change before Mittagessen. Break will be at ten this morning, and school will end at eleven-thirty. That is all. Thank you, Miss Lawrence!"

Miss Lawrence played them out and they went to lessons in a state of wild excitement for the most part. This had been foreseen by the authorities and the entire school with the exception of Nina and the orchestra found themselves in the throes of Spot Tests in every single lesson that morning. This gave no one any time for bad behaviour and Rosalie Dene collected all papers and locked them up until the weekend. They had been only a means to a very desirable end.

Nina came back from her rehearsal in such a state of gloom that Mary-Lou caught her at the first opportunity and demanded to be told what had happened.

"Everything, I should think!" Nina returned in tragic tones. "The entire orchestra broke down twice—and over passages they know quite well! That tall girl from St Mildred's with the glasses—what's her name?—Oh, Stella Johnson!—well, she plays the flute and what she thought she was doing, I don't know; but she began the flute cadenza an octave too high and went squeaking up to the top and then when she couldn't get any higher, she dropped back and you never heard anything so awful! It was like a railway whistle gone mad when she was screeching at her top notes! It's all very well laughing, Mary-Lou, but it isn't *your* responsibility!" Poor Nina heaved a sigh that only just escaped being a groan. "I'm going to make a complete mess of it! I know I am!"

"I don't see why," Mary-Lou said. "After all, you're intending to *play* in public. Why should you mind wagging a little stick in public? It's much the same thing, surely."

"It's no such thing! I'm training to become a professional pianist. I've never done anything at conducting until this term and once or twice last term with the carols. And when it's your own instrument you know it. But now I'm responsible for all the others as well and I *know* I'll give someone the signal to come in at the wrong time!"

"Well, of course, if you go on thinking that way, it's quite likely you will," Mary-Lou said calmly. "You turn right round and snap out of it. You've got to think that you're doing it for poor old Plato—if I know anything of him, he's ramping over this!—and that you're not only *going* to do it, you *can* do it and you're the only one who can."

"It's easy for you to talk!" Nina grumbled. But she went off a little more cheered in spite of herself. Mary-Lou's faith in her helped her and so did the hint that she owed it to Mr Denny to make a success of it.

Mary-Lou departed for the senior common room, having a free period after Break. There, she found Vi Lucy looking as if she had just heard that all her friends and relations had been killed in one fell swoop. It was a rare thing to see Vi looking so melancholy, for she was a cheerful young person as a rule, and Mary-Lou set to work to do what in her lay to dispel the gloom.

"Who's dead?" she demanded as she dropped down on the big settee beside Vi.

"Me—when this awful show is over, I should think!" Vi retorted.

"*You*? I thought the responsibility was Nina's. She's just been unloading to me at some length on those lines, at any rate."

109

"Yes; she conducts and I lead. And a nice mess I made of it this morning! You know, Mary-Lou, Nina's a dear and she's certainly a genius when it comes to her own work. But you have to have something different when you try to hold an orchestra together. Plato has it—besides, we're used to him. But Nina—Oh, I don't know! She doesn't seem to have—to have any *confidence* in herself—or us, either, so far as that goes. It was the *woolliest* affair this morning!"

Mary-Lou eyed her thoughtfully. "In that case, won't you have to play up to her and help her to find it? After all, you're leader."

"I didn't feel much like it this morning, I can tell you. I don't wonder when the Head was choosing the new prees last term she left me out!"

"Vi Lucy, you're a complete goop! You know perfectly well that it was finally decided on a question of age and that gave it to Hilary. Anyhow, I've got some news for you that'll buck you up no end."

"I can't think of anything that would buck me up—except to have this afternoon over," Vi said despondently.

"Don't be such an owl! A bad last rehearsal always means a smashing performance. And I wish," Mary-Lou added in parenthesis, "that I'd remembered to remind Nina of that. She's going round looking as if her last hour has come. However! Have you heard the latest about Amy Dunne?"

"*Amy Dunne*? No! What is there to hear?" Vi demanded.

"She's leaving at the end of this term." Mary-Lou stopped short and eyed her friend hopefully.

"Leaving? *Amy*! But what on earth for?" Vi exclaimed.

"Her elder sister is to be married on the first of June and Amy's to be chief bridesmaid. We don't come back till the first week in May and anyhow, the Dunnes will be running round like frightened hens all that month, I should think. Anyhow, Mr Dunne says it isn't worth her while to come back to school for a fortnight or three weeks and then have the long journey home again, so she wouldn't be

110

coming till the second week in June. Then he decided that when it was all over it would be best for Mrs Dunne to go for a long sea voyage immediately after. She's not strong, you know, and Amy says her mother's going to miss Phyllis terribly. They're going round the world and as Amy was leaving at the end of the year in any case, he's taking her away at Easter. After all, it isn't as if she had Higher or anything like that. She did get through General Cert last year, but it was a bare scrape. She's only going to be at home as her mother needs her. There's nothing, really, to keep her at school. She's eighteen now."

"But she'll be out of all the celebrations! Oh, I do call that hard luck!" Vi cried. "She'll miss the trip to the Tiernsee and everything else. Couldn't they put the voyage off till the end of Juy? It would be only six weeks later at most."

"Amy says not. Says her dad thinks it'll be a good idea to get off right away and give her mother no time to fret for Phyllis," Mary-Lou explained. She was still watching Vi eagerly and that young woman felt it and protested.

"What on earth are you glowering at me like that for? It isn't *my* fault. Anyway, I didn't know you were so pally with Amy."

"I'm not—neither glowering nor specially pally with Amy. I like her all right, but she's a good year older than our crowd and I've never been more than pleasantly friendly with her, and well you know it!" Then, as Vi gave her a puzzled look, her patience gave way. "Oh, Vi! What a goop you are! Don't you *see*? Amy's a pree, isn't she? Her going will leave us one short. There aren't many people to choose from. What's the betting that it's *you*?"

Vi went first white and then red. It had been a big disappointment when she had been left out of the prefect list at the beginning of the school year, though she had never breathed a word about it to anyone. Even now, she only said, "I'm not the only one. What about Jill—or Hilda? And there are Meg and Janet."

"Oh, do talk sense! You're the only possible one!" Mary-Lou retorted. "Jill is so delicate there's never any relying on her, poor kid. Hilda's woolly-minded and too much of a giggler. As for Meg and Janet, no one in their senses would choose them to be prees. Meg's a complete scatterbrain and Janet is so absolutely colourless that half the time you never notice whether she's there or not. A nice prefect *she* would make! You'd have the juniors and middles sending the roof sky high in no time."

Mary-Lou had to stop there, for the bell rang for the end of the period and both were due for translation with Mlle who was famed for her own punctuality and her dislike of latecomers to her lessons. But what she had said had certainly given Vi plenty to think about. She stopped worrying about the pantomime and in the intervals of translating *Le Blocus* dwelt delightedly on the possibility of joining the grandees of the school at the beginning of next term.

The pantomime was due to begin at a quarter to fifteen —or three—and the school were all in St Luke's Hall by half-past one. Some of the elder girls were selling programmes and others were helping with the tea and coffee which would be provided during the interval. The more responsible members of the Middle School would act as messengers and Inter V as a whole were to be ushers.

St Luke's Hall had been built by subscription a couple of years before. Here the friends and relatives of patients in the Sanatorium were entertained by concerts, bridge drives, socials and plays as well as an occasional cinema show. Those patients who were well enough had their own section screened off from the body of the hall and would be attended by the nurses. The hall stood not far from the gates of the big Sanatorium and, for the sake of the invalids, most shows were matinées.

It had a very complete stage with a certain amount of stock scenery, the gift of a well-known actress whose small girl had spent two years at the Görnetz Platz when the Sanatorium was first opened. An American millionaire who owed his life to the care of the staff at the Sanatorium had endowed it and various other grateful people had added gifts of one kind or another so that it was very complete.

Behind the scenes, the St Mildred girls were already in

the dressing-room, changing into their first scene dresses and submitting to being made-up with as Chinese a make-up as possible. The chorus and the ballet fled to their own rooms to get ready and the orchestra gathered gloomily in the tiny room under the stage where the music was kept.

Nina joined them there when she had got rid of her wraps. She looked very young in her gentian blue frock with its spotless collar and cuffs, her mane of straight black hair twisted round her head for the occasion in a pigtail coronal. Despite Mary-Lou's efforts earlier, she was terribly nervous and most of the orchestra were in the same state. Then Vi entered with shining eyes and glowing cheeks, her violin tucked under her arm, her bow in her hand.

"Hello, folks!" she said cheerfully. "Everyone with stringed instruments chalked their pegs? Here's the chalk. Get down to it, all of you! Can't have pegs slipping during the show! I say, Nina!" She drew her into a corner while those of the players who had not attended to it before hurriedly chalked their pegs and then tuned up again.

"Don't you worry, Nina. We're all behind you and we'll back you up to the limit. Anyhow, people will be listening to the panto and not us, so you don't have to think about that." She paused and looked at the other girl. Then she bobbed a curtsey. "I look towards you! Honestly, Nina, I'd no idea you were so good-looking! That hair-do suits you down to the ground."

"Are the doors open yet?" Nina asked, a little of the strain leaving her face.

"Just! That's why I shot back here. Our own crowd are in their seats with a whole bevy of staff to keep them in order. And Jo Scott came down to tell me that Inter V are backing you for all they're worth, Nina, and they know you'll come up to scratch!"

Nina flushed but had not time to reply for Miss Lawrence arrived to say that it was time the orchestra took their places and they had to file out into the orchestra pit where the girls gave them a hearty welcome which was taken up by those members of the audience who were already seated.

113

"What's the time?" Stella of the flute muttered to Gwen Parry who played a cello.

"Just on half-past two, I think—I mean half-past fourteen," Gwen said with a giggle. "Where on earth's Vi?"

Vi arrived to answer this. With her lovely face all aglow with excitement and her chestnut hair gleaming under the lights, she somehow gave even the nervous Stella a moment's respite. As she reached her desk, she leaned forward and hissed to everyone within hearing, "Keep your tails up! This is going to beat the band!" Carefully keeping her face turned from the audience, she grimaced at them all with the result that one or two nearly choked with laughter. Then she sat down and as she did so, Nina appeared in the rostrum. At the same moment, the house lights had been lowered and it was a second or two before the audience who were not in the know, realised that it was a girl who was conducting this time and not the well-known Mr Denny.

Joey Maynard, sitting near the front with Mike and the twins beside her, saw a slim, anxious-faced woman clutch at the arm of the big, red-headed man beside her and caught the whispered, "Guy! It's *Nina*! Nina's conducting!" and grinned to herself, even as the conductor raised her baton, all instruments came to the ready and then the orchestra crashed into the opening phrase of the overture.

Hitherto, St Mildred's had contented themselves with some well-known piece of music, but on this occasion, Mr Denny had composed the overture himself. Nina was determined that if he could not be there to conduct it, it should at least have as good a send-off as she could manage. There was authority in the sweep of her baton and the girls felt it. Vi ceased to experience the feeling that they were not being held together, and played her most brilliant. Stella's flute came ringing above the string accompaniment in the queer eastern phrases the singing master had evolved. The cadenza which had gone so badly in the morning rippled out without a mistake. The gay little overture came swiftly to its close and then, with a final chord, ended. The applause broke out and Nina, her shyness gone now, turned round and bowed gravely to the wild clapping which had been begun on the instant by Inter V who were full of sympathy for the conductor and were all set to prove to her that they really did back her for all they were worth.

Nina gravely bowed again and again. Then she turned to the orchestra, her baton up, and at once they swung into the music for the opening chorus. The curtains went up on the scene of "Widow Twankey's Laundry" and the chorus, all dressed in blue tunics and trousers, with their sleeves well-rolled up rubbed and scrubbed and even mangled as they sang.

Into this cheery scene irrupted the Widow herself, played by Sally Winslow, now in her second term at St Mildred's. She was in blue, too, but her head was literally covered with stick-pins and she carried an enormous fan with which she fanned herself and other people as she spoke her lines. They were one long grumble about the difficulty of the times and the laziness of her only son, Aladdin, who refused to work though she had procured him various jobs, including a newsboy, a bootblack, a chimney-sweep, and a floor-polisher. The soap was bad and people did nothing but complain that when she returned their laundry, it was full of holes. As a final calamity, her last pair of nylons had laddered and now she had to go bare-legged!

Aladdin entered to this tale of woe and a funny scene ensued during which the Widow scolded and tried to beat him with her fan while Aladdin, who was played by Julie Lucy, sister of Vi and cousin to Barbara and Janice Chester, wriggled away and finally ended by upsetting his mother into the tub.

The chorus rushed to help her out and the scene ended with her shaking her fist at her son and threatening him with various awful punishments. The chorus joined in and pelted Aladdin with the articles they were supposed to be washing until, by the time the curtain fell, the stage was covered and Aladdin, seizing his opportunity, picked up his mother and popped her into an enormous clothes-basket which he persuaded two of the laundresses to bear off, what time the lady kicked wildly.

115

As this ended, the orchestra modulated into a tranquil melody and the backcloth of the first scene had vanished when the curtain rose again, to show the garden of the Emperor of China. The ballet swirled in in a mazy dance while the chorus hummed the air behind the scenes with charming effect. The dancers drifted off just as Aladdin appeared, leaning over the top of the wall to look down at the flowery scene below him and the Princess tripped in from the opposite wings, singing a song bemoaning her lonely fate as the Emperor's only child. Halfway through, Aladdin joined in, much to her alarm. She turned to fly, but he leaped down gracefully—incidentally, nearly bringing the wall down with him—and advanced to kneel at her feet and proclaim himself the victim of her beauty.

The Princess was coy, reminding him of the awful fate that awaited any man who should look on her face without her father's permission. Aladdin vowed that even beheading was worth having seen her. In fact, he would welcome death since he could have no hope of claiming her for his bride. The Princess asked why and he told her that he was the son of a washerwoman without a penny to his name. There were a few more graceful speeches from the pair. Then the Princess suddenly clutched at him. She had heard footsteps. The gardeners were coming and if they caught him, he must die by torture. He must get away instantly.

Aladdin, with more common sense than might have been expected, asked how he should do that and she told him to hide in the little summerhouse at one side and she would send away the gardeners. Then he must climb the wall and go away. She hustled him into the summerhouse just in time and the chorus, now clad in Chinese coolie dress, with enormous straw hats on their heads, appeared with garden-brooms, headed by the chief gardener, and singing what was called "The Gardeners' Song."

The Princess waited in front of the summerhouse and when the song was finished, she called to them in peremptory tones. They all turned and in a moment were grovelling on the ground with shrieks of horror. The chief gardener besought her in frenzied tones to hide her face

116

for if the Emperor knew they had seen it, he would have them all executed. At every sentence, the prostrate gardeners wriggled violently and whenever he paused for breath they howled dismally. The Princess waited until he had finished. Then she bade them depart at once. She would say nothing and her father would never know. The gardeners moaned out gratitude and proceeded to wriggle out, still on their faces.

And here an unrehearsed incident took place which reduced the audience to the verge of hysterics. Len was sprawled next to Margot. Like all the rest, they had their long pigtails stitched to the crowns of their big coolie hats. In her wild writhings, Margot somehow managed to swing hers across her and Len, struggling backwards, lay firmly on it. The hats had been fastened to their heads with safety pins and when Margot tried to go on, Len's weight held hat and pigtail and wrenched at her hair so violently that she let out a squeal which made the Princess jump and bump into the side of the summerhouse which was not built for heavy blows and rocked as a result. Aladdin, who had been crouching down, bounced up, exclaiming all too audibly, "Look out! You'll have it over!" Len, the innocent cause of her sister's discomfort, took another wild wriggle backwards, yanking the pigtail with her and both it and the hat came away, disclosing Margot's red-gold head to which she clapped her hands and only the quick movement of Abanazar who was waiting for his entrance, prevented her from giving her triplet an unvarnished opinion of her. Luckily, Abanazar *was* there and he stooped down with the utmost swiftness, caught Margot's ankles and hauled her out of sight almost in one movement. His next was to fling an arm swathed in long bright green sleeves across her face, effectually smothering the first remark on her lips. At the same time he hissed, "Shut up, you little idiot! Not another sound out of you!"

Tears were standing in Margot's blue eyes, for Len's last movement had actually pulled a few hairs out by the roots, but she recollected herself and when Barbara Walton—to give the gentleman his proper name—set her down, she scuttled off to the dressing room, silent, but inwardly resolving to let her sister hear *all* about it once the pantomime was over!

Meanwhile, the leading characters proceeded with the play. Aladdin escaped; the Princess sang a song of farewell to him and the curtains fell to rise a minute or two later on the laundry again, this time with the tubs and wringer standing neatly round the walls while the Widow Twankey sat knitting and singing a song entitled *When My Old Man Was Alive*.

The chorus was also there, sitting on the floor and they joined in the chorus:

"Oh what a glorious time we had
When my Old Man was alive!
Food was cheap and taxation was low
When my Old Man was alive!
We went to a different picture each night;
We billed and cooed—'twas a gorgeous sight!
And everything then seemed to go all right
When my Old Man was alive!"

There came a knocking at the door as this pathetic ditty ceased and Abanazar entered. He wanted lodgings for the night. He also asked if the widow could put him on to an active young man to do a well-paid job for him. She assured him that she could and when Aladdin, very lovelorn and dreamy entered, she attacked him on the subject at once. He had still not wakened properly from his meeting with the Princess and there ensued such a volley of cross questions and crooked answers as reduced the audience to tears of mirth. However, it was straightened out in the end and when the Widow had gone to bed, Abanazar and Aladdin had an interview in which the famous ring was handed over after Aladdin had promised to help the lodger to find his long-lost old lamp.

The pantomime proceeded successfully. Nina proved her worth as a conductor and the music went with a swing. Aladdin found the lamp and had the famous quarrel with the magician. He rubbed the lamp and the genie appeared. Wealth was his and so was the Princess. Then, just when they were swinging up to the climax, the worst thing of all happened.

118

Aladdin and his bride were standing in the wings, waiting as the chorus and the ballet filled the stage for the final scene. The Emperor, very gorgeous in yellow and purple was behind them, the Widow equally gorgeous in pea-green and cerise at his side.

Suddenly the Emperor, a big girl who had come to St Mildred's for a year from a north country boarding school, elevated her nose, muttering, "Funny smell of burning!"

At her words, the other three also sniffed and smelt it at once. Aladdin, with a hissed, "Keep quiet!" turned and rushed off to find someone. At the same moment, from just at the far end of the orchestra pit, there rose, blue and wavering against the glow of the footlights, a thin wisp of smoke. A lady sitting opposite, promptly lost her head and shrieked "Fire!" and made a wild dive to get out.

There was pandemonium at once. Many other people began to lose their heads. Joey Maynard contrived to clutch all three of her children in her arms and heave them up on the seats, standing firm against the shoving of panic-stricken people. The chorus and ballet crowded off the stage and there might have been an ugly incident. But it was just here that Nina came up to scratch in good earnest. Raising her voice and yelling so that the orchestra could hear, she shouted, "Go on playing—go on playing! Don't stop!"

The orchestra got down to it, though more than one of them was shaking with fear. They swept into the final chorus which was written to the tune of, "Come to the Fair," At the same moment, some of the girls, recovering their senses came back to sing and Joey Maynard, white and shaking with fear for her babies, lifted up her golden voice and sang with them fortissimo.

It did the trick! Apart from some score or so of people who were too utterly panic-stricken to respond, the audience stopped fighting and began to move out in more or less orderly fashion, the school setting them the example. Meanwhile, the fire service at the Sanatorium had gone into action, located the fire which was in a small cubbyhole under the stage, and were getting control of it as fast as they could. By the time the last person had left the auditorium, it was practically out and comparatively little harm had been done. Then, and only then, did Nina drop her baton and the orchestra their instruments. Vi glanced up, saw Nina sway, and caught her just in time to break her fall. Miss Annersley and Miss Wilson, who had been jammed by the crowds, also came at this moment, and between them they got the last of the girls out, even as Gaudenz from the school came to announce that all was well.

"Thank God!" burst from the two Heads simultaneously.

Mary-Lou, standing near, her face white from the shock, added her quota.

"And thanks be to Nina! She's proved herself a real heroine. And at least no one's been hurt."

CHAPTER ELEVEN

AN OLD ACQUAINTANCE TURNS UP

IT was the hospital staff who got to the bottom of the affair in the end. Some fairly intensive questioning of everyone concerned finally brought it home to Eitel Schwarz, a gangling lad of sixteen who was, to say the least of it, simple. He did odd jobs about the Sanatorium and had been pressed into service on the day of the pantomime to help with the scene-shifting. He had a weakness for cigarettes and, despite orders that no one was to smoke anywhere in the hall, he had found the cubbyhole, slipped in between scenes, and lit up. Then the call had come for him from his own particular taskmaster, Heinrich, and he had dropped the cigarette, stamping on it in passing, and raced off to do his duty. But the cigarette was not out. It had rolled against a bundle of dusters, still smouldering and the result had been as we have seen. It was fortunate for all concerned that the cubbyhole was aired by a grating set in the front of the stage through which the smoke had escaped, alarming everyone terribly, but at least giving warning of the danger.

Dr Maynard dragged Eitel's confession out of him by means of relentless questioning. Eitel was frightened, but the doctor was not to be put off by his lies and evasions. Finally, the foolish youth broke down and owned up fully.

"I see," Jack Maynard said thoughtfully. "And so, for the sake of indulging an appetite, you risked setting the hall in a blaze and causing any number of deaths and injuries. You did know it was forbidden, didn't you?"

Eitel nodded. Heinrich, knowing his weakness, had warned him twice over that very day.

"Very well," the doctor said briskly. "Of course, after this, we can't trust you so you won't be asked to help with the plays again."

Eitel's face fell. He loved the excitement and the importance of feeling that he had a part in the plays. "Truly, Herr Doktor, I will promise never to do it again," he pleaded; but Jack Maynard was adamant.

"I've just told you we can't trust you. Oh, I know you mean it now; but it might happen again. You might forget and another time, we might not be so fortunate. You might choose somewhere to smoke where there was no chance of the smoke escaping until it was too late. We won't risk it! Further, you are never to smoke during your duty hours. And to make sure that this doesn't happen, in future your wages will be paid direct to your mother. She'll see to it that you don't get enough to spend much on baccy!"

Eitel burst into a howl when he heard this. He was well aware of the fact that the few centimes a week his mother would dole out to him would never go far and certainly there would be very few cigarettes in the future. However, after this punishment, he was told that he might stay on at the Sanatorium, so the worst did not happen as his parents had feared it might.

"The kid's not all there," Jack had said when he was discussing it with the Board. "Also, they're poor enough and need his wages. Odd jobs like ours are about all he can be trusted to do and the school won't have him—and I don't blame 'em, either," he added. "His father gave him

121

a whaling when he got him home and they'll keep an eye on him and see that he gets few smokes after this."

"I'll send down and get some chewing-gum for him," Matron said tolerantly. "If he's got to have bad habits, I'd rather see him chewing like a cow than risk having a fire. He can't do any harm with chewing-gum."

By the time all this happened, Nina was herself again and distinctly horrified to find that among the younger girls, at any rate, she was regarded with the deepest admiration as a heroine of the first order. The seniors felt rather the same way, but they had the sense to keep it to themselves after a few words of praise from Blossom Willoughby evoked an outburst which left that insouciant young lady all standing.

"Just the same," Mary-Lou remarked to a select bevy of prefects when they were alone in the prefect's room, "in my opinion she kept her head marvellously."

"I say, wouldn't it be a good idea if we founded our own medal for acts of bravery—as an addition to the celebrations next term, I mean—*and* make it retrospective," exclaimed Nan, with a sudden burst of inspiration.

"Why?" Amy Dunne asked, startled.

"So that we could get off to a good start, of course. I can think of at least two people who would earn it since we've been here."

"Jo Scott for fishing that little ass Emerence off the edge of the precipice last summer, of course," Mary-Lou said, sitting up and looking alert. "She would certainly be one. Who else?"

"Prunella Davidson for doing fishing of another kind—when that equally asinine kid Margot Maynard fell into Lucerne the term before. And I can think of one other," Blossom observed, cocking an observant eye at Mary-Lou.

"Who's that?" the lady herself asked innocently.

"You my sweetie-pie, for yanking Ferry out of the way of that landslide when we were all up at the glacier last term," Blossom said with a grin.

Mary-Lou went scarlet to the tips of her pretty ears. "Don't be such an idiot! There was nothing brave about *that*! You can be *the* most complete fool, Blossom!"

"I don't know so much about it's not being brave," Elinor said thoughtfully. "You did risk going down with her. Some people would have been so busy trying to get out of the way themselves, they'd have left Ferry to get out of it herself. Neither you nor Hilary did that. Yes, I agree with Blossom. You two *would* qualify for Nan's medal. Why on earth didn't you have this inspiration sooner, Nan?"

"Because it's only just come to me now," Nan retorted. "But there's nothing to hinder me going to Deney with it even now, is there?"

"Nothing, if that's what you feel like," Hilary agreed. "And talking about the celebrations, when do you think the Head's going to let us know about that big idea she mentioned? Time's getting on and she hasn't told us a thing yet."

"Well, she did say she'd have to consult Madame and the rest," Elinor reminded her. "I don't suppose there's been time to hear from everyone yet."

Sybil Russell came into the room at this point, her eyes like saucers. "What *do* you think?" she began without any further preface.

"That you're an idiot of course!" Blossom retorted promptly and with a broad grin.

"I'm no bigger idiot than you!" Sybil retorted in her turn. Then she remembered. "Anyhow, I haven't time to start scrapping with you. I've got news for you—and believe me, it really is *something*!"

"What is it?" Hilary demanded.

Sybil perched herself on the edge of the table. "Well— how many of you remember that term ages ago when we were all juniors at Plas Howell and the Head and Mlle and Bill and Teddy were all smashed up in a ghastly bus accident?"

"Please, teacher, I do," said Blossom raising her hand. "I was Upper IIb at the time and we didn't have an awful lot to do with the rest of the school, but I remember that quite well. We had to have a locum and we got that ghastly Miss Bubb who tried to stop Julie and me and Vi from going to Auntie Nan's wedding—only she got hoofed out before it came off as Bill returned ages before anyone expected her and took over so we didn't need her—and thank goodness, too!"

"I remember, too," Lesley Malcolm chimed in. "That was the term—the term Gay Lambert ran away in the middle of the night and came back with German measles. Don't you remember how all our lot were shoved into the west wing because we hadn't been near the infection so none of us got it?"

Sybil had suddenly flushed at the break in her remarks. She knew well enough that what Lesley had been going to say was, "That was the term Josette had that awful accident and nearly died." As she herself had been largely to blame for it, she shied at any reference to it. Josette had recovered years ago and was as sturdy as a mountain pony now; but it had been a long time before she had fully recovered. She shivered. Then she gave herself a shake and went back to her announcement.

"I remember the German measles scare. What I really came to tell you is that Miss Bubb herself has turned up after all these years. She's up here. I've just seen her."

"*What*?" It came as a chorus. Not many of them had been at the school during that momentous period, but everyone had heard the story of Miss Bubb and Gay Lambert's escapade.

"What's she doing here?" Blossom demanded.

"Don't ask *me*! All I know is that I had to go over to Freudesheim with a note from the Head to Aunt Joey. I couldn't possibly go by the garden way, so I had to take to the road. I saw someone coming round the curve and just as I reached Aunt Joey's gate, who should come up but the great Miss Bubb! She stared pretty hard at me, but I don't think she really knew I was me, so to speak. Anyhow I wasn't having any. I simply slammed the gate after me and tore up to the house."

"Let's hope she isn't moved to investigate and come and pay us a visit!" Blossom said with heartfelt inhospitality. "From all I remember of her, she was the extreme and frozen limit!"

Sybil grinned. "I don't think she's likely to do that—

124

not after all Mummy said to her about the Gay business. Josette was there at the time and heard it all and told me later on. She was most squashing—Mummy, I mean."

"I wonder just why she's up here?" Hilary observed.

"Perhaps she's looking for a new job and is scouting round to see if she can get one with us," Mary-Lou suggested wickedly. She had not come to the school till a year later but, like the rest, she knew the story.

"Talk sense! *Is* it likely she'd ask for a job in a school where she was Head, even if it *was* very *pro tem*.?" Lesley demanded scornfully.

"Besides, why should she connect Plas Howell with the Görnetz Platz?" Nan added. "If she was hoofed out like that, I don't suppose she took any interest in the school's later doings so she wouldn't be likely to know we're out here."

"No, I suppose not. Anyhow, we can't do anything about it. I expect she's just up on a visit," Mary-Lou said with complete placidity.

They had to leave it at that. In any case, the bell for Kaffee und Kuchen rang just then so they streamed off down to the Speisesaal and Miss Bubb and her sins were speedily forgotten.

Joey Maynard arrived at the school that evening in reply to the Head's note. She arrived in the staff sitting-room where most of them were taking coffee and their ease, with her face ablaze with laughter.

"Hello, everyone!" she cried. "Hope I'm not too late, but young Cecil chose to play me up for once. I think there's another tooth due. I'm in for a night of it, I can see, I'm not staying long." She tossed herself down in the chair Kathie Ferrars pushed forward and looked round at them all. "I've some news for you—all of you who are Foundation Stones, anyhow."

"News?" Miss Wilson who was also there, sat erect in the big chair in which she had been lounging comfortably. "I've news for you myself, now I come to think of it. Joey—Hilda—Jeanne—everyone who was with the school at Plas Howell! Guess who's up here!"

"I can answer that in one. Have *you* seen her, too?

125

And I hoped I'd be the one to get in first!" Joey's voice was full of disappointment.

Mlle poured out a cup of coffee and brought it to her "But chérie, of whom, then, do you speak?"

"Miss Bubb!"

"Miss Bubb?" Biddy o'Ryan offered her biscuits. "And who may she be? 'Tis meself has never heard of her at all, at all!"

"Bridget Mary o'Ryan! You *can't* have forgotten that awful woman who came to us *pro tem.* when Hilda and Nell and Jeanne and Dollie Edwards were all smashed to smithereens in that bus accident—or very nearly, anyhow."

Biddy's face lit up. "Her! Of course I remember her! I was at Oxford by then, you may remember, so I didn't come in for the visitation, but I heard all about it. You and Robin and Daisy all saw to that. I'd forgotten all about her. Did you say she's up here? How do you know?"

"Because I've seen her—though she hasn't seen me. I took good care of that!"

"What did you do?" Miss Derwent asked suspiciously.

"I was coming down our drive when I saw her this morning, strolling past. I shot back to the house in short order, I can tell you. I don't often loathe people but I loathed her and still do. Yes; I know it's unchristian, but I do! When did you see her, Nell?"

"When I came over just now. I know it's night, but there's a full moon and it's as bright as day outside. I knew her instantly. I don't fancy she knew me, though—or if she did, she cut me dead."

"Didn't know you, I should say," Joey said. "When she last saw you, you were *the* most washed-out specimen! You were as white as a sheet and your face was lined with pain. If you remember, you'd come back much earlier than you should in reply to my howls for help. You were anything but fit and you looked it!"

"It certainly seems to have made an impression on you," Miss Wilson said mildly. "I'd no idea I looked such a freak! That would account for her not knowing me, then." She glanced complacently at her own reflection in a nearby mirror. Whatever she may have looked like so soon after the accident, no one could accuse her of being anything but a healthy specimen now. There were few lines in her face and her cheeks glowed with health. On the whole, she decided, Joey was right. She looked a good ten years younger than she had looked then.

"What became of her after she left us?" Mlle asked, leaving the coffee-pot to look after itself in her interest.

"Blessed if I know! Didn't she join up with some old pal of hers in a school somewhere in the south of England? I *think* that's what Madge told me," Joey said.

"But surely she must have retired by this time!" Rosalie exclaimed. "She must be going on for seventy. I expect she's come out for a holiday—though what can have brought her to the Görnetz Platz at this time of year is more than I can say! Your guess is as good as mine."

"What's the yarn?" Miss Derwent demanded. "I've never heard of the woman."

"Years before your day! Come to English tea on Sunday and I'll tell you," Joey said instantly. "And that goes for anyone else who wants to hear. We *did* have a time of it! I was teaching junior Latin to help out and Stephen was a baby to complicate matters."

"Well, we haven't time just now for any past history," Miss Annersley said, suddenly taking a hand. "Joey, what does Madge say about the chapels?"

"She thinks it's the best idea of the lot and she and Jem and Dick and Mollie all agree and will forward cheques in due course. So as we are *all* agreed, what about letting the girls know, Hilda? The sooner we make a start, the sooner we can get down to the building itself, you know. I'll hand over my last publisher's cheque and Jack says he'll double it. Has anyone any idea what it's likely to cost?"

"How could we possibly?" Miss Wilson demanded. "It can't be done for nothing, though, so your cheques will all be very welcome. In the meantime, we ought to form a committee to deal with the thing. We'll have to arrange for an architect and find a builder, too. Can your family come over shortly, do you think?"

"They'll have to, won't they? Madge can leave the twins with Marie or Rosa, but Mollie will have to bring Daph with her. Peggy's too young to have charge of a baby. Probably she'll come along as well. When do you want the meeting, Hilda?"

"As soon as possible. Rosalie, I don't know quite what will happen to our correspondence during the next few days, but you'll have to drop everything and see about those circulars. You'd better run down to Interlaken in the morning and take it to the printers. They did promise us a rush order, didn't they?"

"Yes; they said they'd put it through at once. And the seniors will help out with addressing the envelopes."

"Then shall we fix it for next week if Jem can get away? They'll all stay with me, of course. Oh, and everyone! Don't tell the girls Madge is coming! Let her breeze in at prayers one morning and give them a shock!"

"Joey! How old are you? Very well; so far as the girls are concerned they shall only hear that the best of our suggestions is the chapels and we are all beginning to collect subscriptions at once. They need know nothing more until Madge and Co. arrive."

"Why do you want it so quickly?" Miss Wilson demanded.

"Well, as you've all informed me, the sooner we begin collecting, the sooner we can begin on the chapels," Joey said as she stood up and began to swathe herself in the large shawl she had worn to come to the school. "And apart from that, it *would* be a pity if Madge missed Miss Bubb! May I be there to see the meeting between them!" And with this, Joey fled back to her teething daughter, pursued by laughter and calls from her hostesses.

CHAPTER TWELVE

MISS ANNERSLEY MAKES ANOTHER ANNOUNCEMENT

"LEN! Len Maynard! Stop a minute! Miss Annersley wants to see you!"

Len, tearing round the house at top speed, pulled up

short and turned to go slowly back to where Yseult Pertwee stood. "Did you say the Head wanted to see me?"

"Yes; she said I was to tell you to go to the study as soon as morning school is over."

Len nodded. "I see. Thank you for giving me the message," she added very properly in the French which both had spoken, this being Friday and therefore "French" day. Being well aware that Yseult's French was by no means as fluent as her own, she also spoke slowly and clearly and the elder girl flushed up.

"You need not speak to me as if I were an infant," she said sharply. "I can understand you quite well."

Len was feeling wicked. "Oh, good! I'm glad you're coming on so fast," she said rapidly. "It's such hard luck when people are speaking a foreign language all round you and you can't understand even half of what they're saying! Congratulations, Yseult! You *have* made strides this term!"

Yseult could only make out a word here and there, for naughty Len had become richly colloquial and she chattered at a rate that left the elder girl stunned. As soon as she rattled off her speech, she turned and raced off again to find her own clan to whom she broke the news, winding up by demanding, "Why should the Head want me like that? I've done nothing."

"Goodness knows," Emerence said. "It isn't like you to do things that make her send for you like that. What have you been up to?"

Len had been searching her conscience in the intervals of getting on with her work all that morning. She had found it quite clear of any major sin, so she replied promptly, "Nothing—or nothing that matters. It can't be my lessons; I had A for my algebra prep and A+ for French, so it can't be that. And I can't think of a single rule I've broken, either."

"You were whistling on the corridor this morning," Con reminded her sister.

"Yes; and Matey caught me and told me exactly what she thought of me. She would never report me for a thing like that."

"Oh, well, you'll soon know now," Rosamund said soothingly. "There goes the bell for the end of Break. It's only an hour and a half more to wait."

They were all speaking French—more or less. The Maynards, thanks to having had a year in a Canadian-French convent, were fluent in the extreme. Rosamund and Jo had fair vocabularies and their accent was improving. The rest spoke a polyglot mixture when there was no one in authority near enough to hear. They used as much French as they could manage and helped it out with English words pronounced as Frenchily as possible and oddments of Latin and even German on occasion. The full result was enough to make a Frenchman tear his hair if he had heard it—it *did* reduce both Mlle de Lachennais and Mlle Berné to speechlessness on occasion—but at least it wasn't *English*, as Emerence Hope had blandly pointed out to the latter lady when called to order once!

Still chattering, they moved in a body to their splashery where they had to pull off their goloshes, worn for the garden in this weather, hang up their coats and made sure that their hair was not too untidy before they went back to their form room and waited for Mlle de Lachennais to come and give them dictée.

Len was still worrying over Miss Annersley's message and it is on record that she produced a paragraph with seventeen mistakes in it.

"But, petite, this is terrible!" Mlle exclaimed as she scored out word after word. She scribbled D– at the end and Len went very red.

"I'm sorry," she murmured.

"But you know all this! Often have you done dictée with me that is harder and have made not one fault! Are you, perhaps, sick?"

"No; I'm quite well, thank you," Len replied in a mumble.

"Then I do not understand. You must write out each word three times correctly and *never*, but NEVER, show me such work again!" Mlle dismissed the crimson Len to her seat and turned to deal with Betty's effort.

"What's wrong with her?" Margot muttered to Rosamund with whom she shared one of the dual desks to which Inter V had been promoted at the beginning of the year. She had been at her violin lesson during Break so had heard nothing about the Head's message to her sister.

With one eye on Mlle, who might be very jolly out of school but was a strict disciplinarian in, Rosamund hissed. "The Head has sent for her at the end of school."

Margot opened her forget-me-not eyes until they looked as if they might drop out. "But why ever?" she demanded breathlessly.

"She doesn't know—and neither do we."

Margot thought quickly. "I bet it's about that idea of hers she sent up for celebrating our coming of age," she said. Then Mlle dismissed Betty who had gone one better than Len with eighteen mistakes so she had to subside.

When the lesson was over, Mlle had gone and they were waiting for Miss Ferrars to come to them for physical geography, she voiced her idea aloud and Len's face instantly cleared. "Of *course*! I might have thought of that for myself! What a goon I am! I couldn't think what I'd done and it worried me so that I couldn't do anything with that dictée and so I lost my marks and that'll pull me down all right in form! Oh, I could kick myself for being such an ass!"

"I wonder what she's decided?" Joan Baker said; and then Miss Ferrars arrived, rather breathless, since she had been detained by Miss Wilson and was late, and set to work to show them how to plot out the contours of mountains.

It is safe to say that where most of them were concerned, most of her words went in at one ear and out at the other. Margot's guess had excited them to the limit and they could scarcely wait until it was time for Len to go to the study. Miss Ferrars quickly realised that it was a case of pearls before swine in their present mood and stopped adorning the blackboard with various figures. She had learned a good deal in her term and a half of teaching and now she set a trap for them. Cleaning the board, she drew the outline of a mountain, marking the various contours at every fifty feet. When she had finished, she dusted the chalk off her hands and then said blandly, "And now we'll see how much you have learned so far. As you will observe, I have marked off the contours at a hundred feet. Draw the figure showing this and pay particular attention to the sharpness or otherwise of the rise." Then she sat down at her table, and began to look through IVa's maps of Australia, having sown consternation among them.

Inter V looked first at her and then at each other with horror. What *did* they do with the thing? Of the entire nineteen, only three had taken in enough to set to work without further help. The rest had been miles away and hadn't attempted to take in anything of what the mistress had said.

With a vague memory of the beginning of the lesson, Len drew something shaped like a bean and labelled it "100 ft.". What did she do now? She sucked the end of her pencil and stared round the room. No inspiration there!

Miss Ferrars looked up and caught her wandering gaze. "Have you finished, Len?" she asked gently.

"Er—no, Miss Ferrars," Len admitted with great reluctance.

"Then please go on and don't gaze about you. If you have listened to me, it should be quite easy. You have only to follow my instructions. Eve! Have you finished? No? Then please stop sucking your pencil and go on!"

Eve, as red as Len, removed her pencil from her mouth and transferred her gaze to her rough-book. She had even less idea than the latter young lady what to do, so it ended with her still staring and wondering how, exactly, you did do contours.

Miss Ferrars gave them exactly ten minutes. Then she rapped on her table and told them to put their pencils down. She passed quickly round the room, examining the work. Exactly three people seemed to have listened to her. Jo Scott had made a very fair shot at it, but that was to be expected from Jo who generally managed to keep her attention on her work. Rosamund Lilley had also done pretty well. As for Con Maynard, she had been away with Matron, paying a visit to the dentist and had only come into the room after the mistress had begun her lesson. She had been out of school most of the morning and knew nothing of the latest, so she had worked steadily and her diagram was quite good for a first attempt. As for the rest, their pages were either quite empty or showed the same sort of drawing as Len's. Miss Ferrars drew her pencil firmly through the lot and returned to the blackboard.

"I don't know what is wrong with you girls," she said, "but you stay here until you manage to draw me a reasonably accurate diagram. I will go through the lesson once more. Please pay attention. Anyone *not* doing so will report herself for detention at the end of the afternoon and come in on Saturday morning."

As this meant not only losing the Saturday morning ramble, but also losing an order-mark and, if one had two others, all the Saturday evening fun into the bargain, she had no need to speak again. The girls listened with all their ears and by the time she had finished—which was a few minutes before the end of the lesson, even Yseult had contrived to grasp what she wanted. She set them preparation, then gathered up her books and departed, leaving them all breathing rather more freely.

The last lesson that morning was literature with Miss Derwent. They had begun work on a Shakespeare play this year for the first time. Miss Derwent chose to ignore the speech out of *A Midsummer Night's Dream* which they had learned and told them they would go on reading. This was always fun, for they had their own special parts, given out at the beginning of the Christmas term, and the mistress had a very pleasant habit of letting them do a full scene before stopping to ask if they wanted any explanations which she gave in full. Even Yseult looked forward to this lesson. They had reached the scene where "the rude mechanicals" of Athens first rehearse their play and they enjoyed it thoroughly. Indeed, there were quite a few groans when the bell rang for the end of morning school and they had to stop.

"Mayn't we go on with it next lesson, Miss Derwent?" Rosamund Lilley asked eagerly.

Miss Derwent laughed. "I *ought* to hear you in that speech of Helena's you're supposed to have learned for me. Suppose you write it out from memory for prep? If it's correct, we'll go on reading. If too many of you don't know it, I'm afraid we must concentrate on that. It's in your own hands."

She left the room, laughing, and then Len remembered that she had to go to the Head.

"Am I decently tidy?" she asked anxiously.

"Let's have a look at your hands," Jo said, taking charge as form prefect. "My good kid, if you go to the Head with hands like that she'll ask if you've been having a bath in the ink! Scram and wash them. And you'd better do something to your hair while you're busy. You look *wild*!"

Len made a face at her before she fled from the room, but she had the sense to pay attention to Jo and it was a very proper-looking schoolgirl who finally presented herself in the study. Every hair was in place and her hands were spotless. Miss Annersley greeted her with a smile and Len's nervousness vanished.

"Come along, Len," the Head said. "I sent for you to tell you that everyone likes your suggestions for our coming of age celebrations, so tomorrow I'm going to announce it after prayers. But as it is *your* idea, I thought it your right to know about it first."

Len was pink. "Oo—oh! How marvellous! Auntie Hilda, can I tell our crowd?"

"*Can* you?" the Head asked with a certain inflection which everyone who used this particular form of bad English knew.

Len giggled. "Well, *may* I? Sorry, Auntie Hilda! I forgot!"

"It's time it was habit with you. Yes; you may tell your own clan, seeing they helped you to work it out. Say nothing to anyone else, though."

"Oh, *marvellous*!" Len clasped her hands. Her violet-grey eyes shone and her pointed face was pink with excitement.

Miss Annersley surveyed her thoughtfully. Like her

134

sisters, Len had been a very pretty little girl. At present, she was growing fast and was too thin and coltish for beauty, but, the Head decided, it was all there. By the time she was sixteen or seventeen, Len would be a very good-looking young person. Meantime her English certainly needed some attention.

"Len," she said gently, but with a keen edge under the gentleness that jerked her hearer to attention, "when your mother was your age, everything with her was either "tophole" or "topping". With you, it seems to be "marvellous". Please try to find a few more adjectives to express pleasure or delight. As you know, I object to repetition. Not only is it bad style; it can become intensely boring and monotonous. English is one of the richest languages there is and there should be no need for you girls to confine yourselves to three or four adjectives in the way you do. Please find some others." She stopped there and favoured her pupil with a sudden smile. "Now you may go and tell your news. And don't forget what I've just said about your language, please."

"Yes, Miss Annersley; and thank you very much," Len said primly. Then she gave the Head a grin as she made for the door where she curtsied and then went scuttering off to the common room in search of her clan.

Left to herself, the Head laughed outright. "I *ought* to call her back and remind her that racing about the corridors like that is against the rules," she thought as she stood up and tossed off her gown. "I think I'll let it go this time. How like Joey she is growing! More so, I think, than either of the others, even though Con has her mother's colouring and Len hasn't. It's rather fun watching the second generation developing like this. I wonder what that child will do when she's older?"

Meanwhile, Len had torn back to join the others and was able to relieve the minds of her own clan by hissing, "C'est bien! Je le raconterai à vous tout plus tard!" which calmed them for the time being. At least there was no trouble on hand.

When she could, she got her crowd together and told them what the Head had said.

"May we tell the rest now, then?" Emerence asked eagerly in her shaky French.

"She said not—not till she's announced it after prayers tomorrow. And look here, everyone! We'll have to be very careful about fines for the future."

"Why?" Margot asked, wide-eyed.

"We want to give as much as we can to the fund to build the chapels, don't we? If we have to be always paying fines for slang or forgetting to use the language for the day—well, you know what it does to our pocket-money, be careful, all of you. Oh, and the Head says we're to find some other adjectives besides "marvellous". She says it's bad style and monotonous and that English is a rich language so we ought to be able to find something else," Len reported. She had certainly inherited her mother's flypaper memory.

The rest listened with resigned expressions. It was odd that people were always making a fuss about their English. However, they supposed they would have to see to it. Margot nodded as a bright idea came into her head.

Con got there first, however. "I'll go through the dictionary," she offered. "I daresay I can find quite a number of new adjectives. I'll make a list and we can use them when I've done that."

"I'll help you," Margot said. "After all," virtuously, "we don't want anyone to have the chance of saying that our English is bad style and—what was the other thing you said, Len?"

"Monotonous," Len repeated, her eyes dancing wickedly. "Good idea, Con! Find us a few out-of-the-ordinary ones while you're busy."

"What do you expect?" Con retorted in injured tones. "You wait!"

"If you ask me," Emerence remarked, reverting to the question of the chapels, "we seem to have let ourselves in for something. Won't it do if Daddy just sends a cheque to the fund?"

"No it won't!" Margot said sharply. "That would be his giving. We want it to be *ours*. Oh, I hope he *will* send a cheque. But you must give your own share, too."

"I've had an idea," said Rosamund in her stumbling French.

"What is it?" they demanded in a chorus.

"Let's reckon how much we have to give in fines each term and try to keep free from them and each week put that week's amount aside from our pocket-money. Then, at the end of the term, we can hand it in."

"Oh, good idea!" Jo exclaimed. "But wouldn't it be better to put it into a box or something every week. You know how it is when you have a little extra saved up. You suddenly see something you want and you forget and buy it and then your money is gone." She carefully refrained from looking at the two people most likely to do this, but Margot and Emerence both reddened.

"Let's do it!" Len cried. "If it belongs to all of us, no one can spend it."

"It will be hard work for me," Emerence pointed out. "I get more fines than anyone else except Margot and even she isn't so bad as I am about slang and she doesn't often get fines for not speaking the right language. That's what comes of you three being in Canada!" She ended with a deep sigh.

"That isn't much help where German's concerned," Len told her. "Well, do we all agree? We get a box from somewhere and put in fine money on each Saturday."

However, that part of it proved needless. Next day after prayers, Miss Annersley told the school about the proposal to build the two little chapels and the girls greeted the idea with wild enthusiasm.

"Just a moment!" she begged when they were finally restored to order. "You do all understand, don't you, that to do such a thing means collecting a very big sum. Building is a costly matter these days. Friends and Old Girls will help, I know. All our present mistresses will help, too, and so will former ones. But you girls must also do your best and it must not lessen our subscriptions to the Sanatorium. That mustn't suffer for this new idea. So if we do it, you must be prepared to sacrifice some of your sweets and other luxuries in order to give. And to help you, I am getting boxes for each form room. You can drop in your offerings and at the end of each week, Miss Dene will open the boxes, make a note of what each contains and put up a list on the notice board in Hall. At the end of term, she will put up a special list to show you how much each form has collected during the term. We'll go on next term, too, and perhaps when the summer holidays come, we may have enough in the bank to justify us in beginning on the foundations. What do you say?"

There was a minute's silence, for most of the girls had not had time to realise that the new proposal must definitely mean self-sacrifice on their parts. Miss Annersley waited while they considered. Then Elinor, having raised her eyebrows at her colleagues and received nods from every one, stood up.

"The Sixth are all prepared to do that, Miss Annersley," she said.

"And so are we!" cried Josette Russell, leaping to her feet and speaking for Va.

Vb were also agreeable, and Inter V were already prepared, for during the previous evening the Maynards and Co. had discussed it with their peers and found most of them willing to join in. Jo Scott announced it very properly and the rest of the form prefects followed suit. It was clear that everyone was agreed. Perhaps the Head's idea of putting up weekly lists of the sums obtained helped to make up their minds. More than one girl resolved just then to avoid as many fines as possible and give up her sweets and other indulgences for the time being so that *her* form might have a chance of heading those lists.

"Very well!" Miss Annersley said briskly when the last of the little girls had spoken. "Then I'll send for the boxes today. Now I have one other announcement to make. I may say that we—I mean all of us who are on the staff— are in full accord. This is that we should have our own medal for acts of special bravery. Herr Laubach is very enthusiastic and has suggested that you might provide the design for it from among yourselves. On Tuesday evening, he will give an illustrated lecture on medals and coins to all the seniors and anyone else who cares to come. The week after, he will devote our art lessons to helping you to develop your own ideas."

She paused and there came a thunderous clapping. When

138

she felt they had relieved their feelings enough for the time being, she stopped them and went on.

"As the medal is to be given retrospectively—that is," she smiled down at the juniors who were looking puzzled by the strange word—"it will be given for any deeds of bravery that have been done since we came to the Oberland. It will be awarded at the end of next term to those girls who have deserved it. I will read you the names of the three we have chosen so far—Prunella Davidson, who rescued Margot Maynard when she fell into Lucerne last March; Josephine Scott, who saved Emerence Hope from falling over a precipice last summer term; Mary-Lou Trelawney whose alertness and forgetfulness of self saved Miss Ferrars from being swept down to the glacier in a landslide last term——"

"Please!" It was Mary-Lou who interrupted with a face like a beetroot. "I don't honestly think I deserve anything for just hanging on to Miss Ferrars. But if I *do* then Hilary Bennet should as well, for she helped, too."

The rest of the school gaped—and so, to be frank, did one or two of the mistresses, though Miss Denny, sitting between Mlle and Nancy Wilmot, murmured, "It's not impertinence; it's just Mary-Lou!"

The Head smiled. "You're quite right, Mary-Lou. Hilary shall have a medal as well. Now sit down and let me finish."

Mary-Lou subsided perforce, for Hilary and Vi pulled her down to her seat with such vim that the thud as she sat, could be heard all over the room! Miss Annersley bit her lip and then went on swiftly.

"That is all I have to say for the present, girls. We are very late with the first lesson, so please settle in as soon as you reach your form rooms. Thank you, Miss Lawrence!"

Miss Lawrence must have been affected by the general excitement, for when she crashed ino the usual march, it was "See the conquering hero comes!" and the school was one broad grin as it marched out and the four who were to be honoured were, as their delighted form-mates did not fail to assure them later, all colours of the rainbow!

CHAPTER THIRTEEN

EXPEDITION FOR INTER V

As there would be so many exciting events during the summer months, it had been decided that this term there should be no proper half-term weekend. Each form was to be given a full day's excursion somewhere and each mistress would have a full weekend off. That had to content them and, in view of all that seemed likely to happen during the summer, most folk were quite satisfied.

"It isn't as if you could expect steady good weather this term, anyway," Betty Landon said wisely to a group of Inter V one evening when they were all hard at work on various objects for their stall at the Sale of Work which was to take place during the celebrations weekend. "Oh, I know we had fun at Zürich last year. But do you remember what the Sunday was like? Pouring rain and a gale of wind and we couldn't put our noses out-of-doors. I'd a lot rather have just this one outing on a fine day and add the rest of the time to the Tiernsee weekend next term. It'll be summer then, and some chance of decent weather."

Her hearers all agreed with this and most of the school were of the same way of thinking, though Amy Dunne bemoaned the fact that she was being done out of a proper half-term this term and would have left before the Tiernsee trip took place.

"But you have had the trip to Neuchâtel this term and you're having the world cruise in June. What more do you want?" Blossom asked with point.

"You can't have *every*thing!" Hilary Bennet added.

Amy looked doubtful and Elinor wisely changed the topic of conversation.

On the Monday morning Rosamund Lilley was down first of all Inter V. She gave a glance at the notice board in passing and then uttered a yell which brought Len

Maynard, Jo Scott and Joan Baker who had followed her into their common room, round her in short order.

"Our expedition!" Len shrieked. "Where are we going?"

"It doesn't say," Jo said, scanning the brief notice carefully.

By this time, a good many other people had arrived and were all milling round in such a way that it was small wonder that those on the outskirts of the mob complained bitterly that they couldn't see.

"Shut up a minute, all of you!" Jo ordered. "I'll read it aloud for you."

They calmed down and she read, " 'The excursion for Inter V will take place, weather permitting, on the coming Saturday. The usual conditions are attached.' There! That's all it says. And it's time this form remembered that it's Monday!" she added, changing rapidly to German. "You've all spoken in English, so far! And so have I, and I've got in first!" She grinned at them and turned from the board triumphantly.

They left it, too, and scattered about the room, some to collect their music and make for the various music-rooms; others to their form room to glance over repetition or New Testament in readiness for the morning's lessons. But all wildly excited and it needed Jo's warning about fines to keep some of them within bounds. However, for the whole of the week Inter V behaved, to quote their form mistress, like a flock of unfledged angels. No one came within any distance of an order-mark. All work was done with the utmost care, even Yseult deciding to fall in with everyone else on this occasion.

The result was that when Saturday morning came, the whole nineteen were able to turn up at seven o'clock Frühstück, looking very smug and pleased with themselves. Miss Ferrars, who would be in charge with Mary-Lou and Hilary to help her, chuckled to herself as she entered to take her seat at the head of the table.

"You look like the good girls from a Victorian story-book," she told them. "I hope you're going to be more interesting companions than that, though. Come along, Mary-Lou and Hilary! Those two chairs are left for you—if you can squeeze in!'"

The two prefects squeezed in and set to work on their porridge.

"Where are we going, Miss Ferrars?" Mary-Lou asked when her bowl was empty.

"To one of the very oldest Swiss cities," Miss Ferrars told her.

"Oh? Which is that?"

"Can't you think?"

"I haven't an idea," Mary-Lou said frankly. "What about Basle?"

"No; it isn't Basle. And hurry up with your breakfast, everyone. We want to catch the five to eight train down, you know."

Mary-Lou glanced at her; decided that it was no use and asked amiably if they were going by train or road?

"By road. A little coach will meet us outside the Ost-Bahn in Interlaken." Kathie Ferrars saw the excited faces and suddenly relented a little. "I'll tell you this much. We're going north of Berne—but it isn't Basle though it's a city on the Aare. I'm sure you'll all love it. Miss Wilmot and I went there for a weekend last term and fell in love with it. Now that's all I'm going to say until we're in the coach, so don't waste your breath doing any more asking—Miss Wilmot! Where are *you* going that you've come down to early breakfast?"

"I'm coming with you after all," Miss Wilmot said. "My extra coaching is off. Lesley has had a session of toothache most of the night, poor girl, and is going down to the dentist this morning. Matron called in at my room to let me know, so I decided to make the most of it and come with you."

"Oh, good!" Kathie Ferrars and Nancy Wilmot were very good friends and it would certainly be more fun for the younger mistress to have one of her colleagues with her. "Come and sit down beside me. One of you folk—

oh, thank you, Jo!" as that young lady arrived with spoon and bowl of steaming porridge for Miss Wilmot.

Miss Wilmot also thanked Jo and set to work to clear her bowl. By the time the girls had finished and were ready for grace, she was on her last roll and the party finally left in plenty of time for the rack and pinion train that would carry them down to Interlaken. A number of the others were at the door or in the short drive to see them off.

"Where are you going?" Isabel Drew hissed at Con Maynard as they went past.

"No idea! Ferry won't tell until we're down," Con muttered. "Tell you later."

Isabel laughed and waved her hand before turning to go back into school. IVa had had their trip a fortnight before.

"I *wish* you'd tell us where we're going," Len said to Miss Ferrars as they slid down the mountainside. "It's so—so tantalising not to know."

Nancy Wilmot chuckled. "Mean to say you don't know yet? Dear me! How sad!" she remarked; and the entire form *and* the two prefects could have shaken her!

However, Miss Ferrars stuck to it and it really was not until they were in the little coach which held twenty-two passengers and rolling along the Hoheweg towards Lake Thun that she finally told them.

"We're going to Solothurn," she said then when every one was settled.

"Where, exactly, is it?" Joan Baker asked. "I don't think I've heard of it."

"*Joan*! It's on the Aare, due north of Berne where we're stopping for elevenses. Only it'll be tenses today, I should think. Miss Annersley is treating you all to coffee and cream cakes."

"Oh, enchanting!" exclaimed Len.

The two mistresses stared at her and then raised their eyebrows at each other. They were not to know that Inter V had taken the Head's remarks about English to Len very seriously and had spent quite a good deal of time with dictionaries that week, hunting out equivalents for "marvellous" and learning them by heart. But they were to experience quite a number of shocks as a result that day.

"We'll have Mittagessen in Solothurn, then?" Jo asked.

"Yes; and Kaffee und Kuchen as well. We're spending the entire day there and even so, you won't be able to see a quarter of what Solothurn has to show!"

"What is there?" Margot asked eagerly. "Any animals?"

"No; no zoo. But there's a very beautiful cathedral and the arsenal which has some quite interesting things in it"—the two mistresses exchanged glances at this and then both giggled wholeheartedly, rousing intense curiosity among their pupils—"and beside that, there are a number of lovely fountains and a museum and in the Marktplatz, there's a clock with figures like the Zeitglockenthurm in Berne. Then there are parts of the old walls and the great Franciscan Friary. There's plenty to see, quite apart from the beautiful old buildings you meet everywhere in the Old Town."

"It sounds completely charming," Rosamund said politely.

"Too sweet for words!" Emerence chimed in. "I think it's going to be a glorious expedition. Miss Ferrars?"

"Well?"

"Why is it that in almost every city in Switzerland they seem to have fountains by the dozen? Just look at Berne! And Zürich has lots. And now you say Solothurn has lots, too. Why?"

"Because it's possible with all the lakes and rivers hereabouts. They have plenty of water and I suppose long ago when they wanted to celebrate some event or great person the usual idea was to erect a fountain. And don't forget that the Swiss are a very artistic nation with great carvers and you know how lovely their fountains can be."

"And how gruesome!" Mary-Lou put in. "What about the Ogre's Fountain in Berne?"

"Ogre's Fountain?" Yseult asked, interested at this.

"Yes; a huge ogre surrounded by fat babies in the act of devouring one another. Ugh! Disgusting! And yet,

144

round all that there's the jolliest ring of dancing bears imaginable! It really is worth seeing if you ever get the chance, Yseult."

"Why was it erected?" Yseult asked. "Did they think that at one time there had been an ogre in that district?"

"Of course not. As a matter of fact, I remember some-one telling us that it was erected beside the city old ditch to frighten the children away. It was pretty deep, you know—the ditch, I mean—and none too safe. So they put up this hair-raising monster—and, I don't doubt, told the kids that if they played around there the ogre would get them sometime."

Emerence had been listening. Now she broke in. "Surely you don't believe in ogres and all that sort of rot, Yseult? At *your* age!"

Yseult flushed. "*I* may not; but people did in the Middle Ages. Look at all the trials for witchcraft!"

"Yes; but that was mainly because frequently people called witches and wizards knew much more than ordinary folk and they were frightened and that made them cruel. Miss o'Ryan once told us in history that fear is oftener at the bottom of cruelty than anything else."

"Anyhow," Hilary put in, "we don't have to worry about witches or ogres or anything of that kind nowadays. Are we visiting the cathedral and the arsenal, Miss Ferrars?"

"Oh yes; you must certainly see those if nothing else. Now look out at Thun. Did you ever see anything bluer in your lives?"

"Yes—the Tiernsee," Nancy Wilmot interjected. "You've yet to see that, my dear. Not that Thun isn't very lovely," she added, "but the Tiernsee really is something! You people," she addressed the girls, "have a treat in store for you!"

"I sometimes feel I can't wait for it!" Len said ecstatically.

"It'll come," Miss Wilmot said laughing. "Only a month or two to hold your horses, Len, and then you'll see it. Hasn't your mother told you about it?"

"Reams!" returned Margot decidedly. "And about Briesau where the school used to be and the Sonnalpe where the San was. She's going to try to go when we do, Miss Wilmot, and then she can show us lots of places she's told us about."

"Is she indeed? Then if I can possibly manage it, I'm coming when you do. To see the Tiernsee again in company with Joey will be a real treat," Miss Wilmot declared. "Not that it'll be the same thing as it used to be—can't be. For one thing, they've turned it into a reservoir to supply part of Tirol with water and they've built a dam across the Seespitz end. I know that for a fact. Still, I daresay we'll be able to recognise quite a lot of it. They drowned out Buchau and Geisalm and one or two of the other tiny hamlets round the lake but not, thank goodness, Briesau, which is where the school was. All the same, we shall see big changes."

By this time, they had left the shore road round Lake Thun and were running northwards towards Berne. The girls looked out eagerly at the plain which was so different from their usual surroundings. They flashed past little farms, villages where people were busy, and through some small towns full of bustle. Then they reached the southern suburbs of the capital and, as Rosamund vowed, had pulled up near a big restaurant almost before they could realise that they had left the countryside and were in the city. Miss Ferrars jumped out and waited until the girls were all out beside her, Miss Wilmot trailing on behind Mary-Lou and Hilary. The driver drove off to seek his own refreshment and they entered the restaurant where they were feasted on coffee with featherbeds of whipped cream floating on top and Berner Leckerli, a kind of spiced honey cake with a thin coating of icing, topped by a white sugar bear for decoration.

"Here's richness!" Hilary sighed as she bit into hers. "Rather a change from our usual milk and biscuits, eh, Mary-Lou?"

Mary-Lou waited to wipe the whipped cream moustache off her lips before she replied. "Richness all right.

I love it for a treat, but I don't think I'd like it as a general thing. Much too sick-making!"

"Mary-Lou, do *not* use that horrible expression!" Miss Wilmot cried. "Though I agree that you'd probably all require castor oil or Gregory powder if we feasted you like this every day," she added with a gurgle.

Miss Ferrars kept an eye on the time. They still had to reach Solothurn and the Head had advised her to allow only half an hour for elevenses. She gave the girls due warning and when the time was up, they poured out of the restaurant into the street to find their coach waiting for them; scrambled in again and set off on the last part of their journey.

"Not that this will take so long," Miss Wilmot observed when the door was shut and they were off. "All the same, we've got to get clear of the city before he can let her out at all and we seem to be caught in a traffic-jam."

"We're off again," Miss Ferrars said as they began to crawl forward once more. "Oh, thank goodness!" For the driver had swung off down a side-street and now they were beginning to make a little way. "The main streets of Berne are *not* any use to people who want to get on—not at this time of day!"

But the driver was experienced and knew his way. They turned along another side-street, crossed the Aare by a wide bridge and came out into the northern suburbs where they passed pleasant houses with little gardens in front which were still bare but gave promise of being very gay before long. Then they left these behind and were speeding along the autobahn which led to Solothurn.

"What a straight road!" Len exclaimed as she peered out of the front window and saw it stretching straight ahead. "It doesn't seem to have a curve in it!"

"The snow's going jolly quick here," Rosamund said critically. "That field we just passed was almost all green. I shan't be sorry. I've loved it but I'm beginning to get tired of it now. It's gone on such a *long* time!"

"Well, you know what it's like next term," Jo said.

"It goes on getting hotter and hotter and then people begin to wish we could have the snow again."

"Not me!" Rosamund said with decision. "I love the hot weather!"

Betty, in the other front seat with Alicia, suddenly gave a delighted squeak. "Lots of houses—and I'm sure I can see the sun on water. That's Solothurn, isn't it, Miss Ferrars?"

"Solothurn it is! Gather up your things, girls, and remember that if you leave anything behind, you'll have to do without it till we go back. The coach is leaving us here till half-past seventeen when it picks us up in the Marktplatz."

The girls stood up to rescue their belongings from the racks, and when they sat down again Miss Wilmot drew their attention to the wall of the Weissenstein, one of the loftier summits of the Jura, forming a solemnly picturesque background to the old city with its tree-lined lanes and many gardens.

"I thought the Juras were in France!" Eve Hurrell exclaimed.

"So they are, for the most part. But this bit is in Switzerland," Miss Ferrars said.

"Anyway, here we are at the Marktplatz. Out you get and for pity's sake don't make too much noise. When you girls are excited, you chatter like a flock of starlings! Solothurn is a quiet little town and we don't want to give the residents a bad shock! Remember you're all in uniform!"

The door was slid open and the girls tumbled out quickly, joining up in their various sets. Jo Scott, with the Maynards, Rosamund and Joan Baker, glanced round and saw Yseult standing alone. Even after nearly two terms, the girl had made no real friend. It was principally her own fault, for she felt far too grown-up to condescend to people who were two or three years younger than herself. She was not nearly advanced enough for promotion to a higher form and so far she had declined to put in the necessary work if that was to happen. So she had to stay

148

down with the younger girls and had never yet risen above tenth in the form. Still, that was no reason why she should be left out, so Jo called to her to come and join their party. The mistresses were arranging with the driver about the return and the two prefects were in the middle of a group composed of Betty, Alicia, Heather Clayton, Charmian Spence and Iris Woodley and had not noticed that Yseult was by herself.

"Yseult! Come on and join our lot!" Jo called. "Room for another and we can't go round in a surging mob and no one wants to croc if they needn't."

Emerence, who had been separated from her special chum, Margot, now raced up and Yseult, after a look round, came slowly to join Jo's party. She had hoped Mary-Lou and Hilary would link up with her as they three were the oldest there, but those young women were fully occupied.

Then Miss Ferrars left the coach and came forward. "Now then! The Münster first," she said. "Mittagessen after that and then we'll go to the arsenal and after that, we'll see what time we have left and what we most want to do with it. Need you croc, Mary-Lou? No, so long as you don't make exhibitions of yourselves; and keep within sight and sound of Miss Wilmot and me. Ready? Then go ahead, Jo and the rest. Across the Market and down that street and we'll come to the Münster in a few minutes."

"And I hope," Nancy Wilmot said in an aside as they came at the end of the little groups of girls, "that your history is better than mine or we'll be in deep waters in less than two minutes. The questions those girls can ask!"

Kathie Ferrars laughed. "I spent the whole of yesterday evening reading up the guide-book we got when we were here before," she retorted. "I'm prepared for them. Mercy! Look at those stragglers! Come on! You *would* come, so now you may do your duty!" And she was off to chase Charmian and Francie back on to the pavement with a sharp reminder that they must keep with the rest or else march in line.

CHAPTER FOURTEEN

SOLOTHURN

"I *say*! It's rather miraculous, isn't it?" This was Len, who was still strictly obeying the Head by avoiding much use of the word "marvellous" with startling results on occasion. She stood stockstill to gaze up at the front of Solothurn's cathedral and the rest of her gang copied her. "Just look at all those statues in their niches!" she continued, pointing.

"And see the fountains on either side of the steps!" Margot added. "What are the statues, Miss Ferrars?"

"Moses striking the rock to bring water, and Gideon wringing out the fleeces that were wet with dew," her form mistress told her.

"Oh! Both something to do with water. That's a good idea!" Jo put *her* word in.

"What a terrific flight of steps to the cathedral!" exclaimed Heather Clayton. "However many are there?"

"Count them and see," Miss Wilmot suggested. "Come along, girls! Up we go!"

The girls raced up the steps, counting as they went, and Betty, the sprinter of the party, announced when she had reached the top, "Thirty-three! Well, they say a baby should go upwards when it's brought to be baptized so that it can rise in the world. I should say that any baby baptized here ought to end up by being a millionaire or something like that!"

"Only you have it wrong," Kathy Ferrars said, laughing as she reached the top. "It's the first steps a baby is taken. I know of one case where there were no steps higher than the bedrooms and the nurse stepped up on a footstool before she took a new baby for its first outing. But it's just an old superstition, Heather. And now we've settled that, look at this front, girls."

"It's magnificent!" Mary-Lou remarked. "What period is it?"

"Italian Renaissance. It dates from 1762," Nancy Wilmot informed her.

"Nothing like as old as the town, then. Didn't you say that was over two thousand years old, Miss Ferrars? Why were they so long in building a cathedral?"

"Oh, this is the new cathedral, built on the foundations of the first one which was erected in the eleventh century. And that, since you're so keen on age, Mary-Lou, is said to have been put up on the site of a Roman temple dedicated to Apollo."

"Oh, I see. Yes; that *does* take it back a long way," Mary-Lou agreed.

Alicia Leonard suddenly said, "You know, it reminds me just a little of St Peter's at Rome. There are the Spanish Steps there, and St Peter's has a dome something like this, too."

"The architect was an Italian by extraction, though he came from the Ticino," Kathie Ferrars, who had been glancing through her guide-book explained. "His name was Guido Pisoni. The interior matches this and it was done by the brothers Francesco and Carlo Pozzi. Come along inside and we'll look round though we can't take all the time we ought, I'm afraid."

They entered and went round, admiring the statues and memorials. Miss Wilmot pointed out the beautiful frescoes on the vaulted roof, the work of yet another member of the Pozzi family and of Gottfried Goetz, and then they went to the sacristy to see the wealth of treasure kept there. The girls were thrilled with it all and it was hard work to drag them away. But time was hurrying on, so the two mistresses hardened their hearts and insisted and presently they were all streaming down the steps, chattering eagerly about all they had seen.

"Eleven altars!" Margot Maynard cried. "And some of them are simply lovely!"

"I thought the pictures were beautiful." Yseult observed.

"But it seems a pity not to have them in a picture gallery where they could be seen in a good light."

"But they were painted *for* the cathedral. You couldn't possibly move them!" Len argued. "They were done for God's house and if you shoved them into a picture gallery, it wouldn't be the same thing at all."

"I suppose you're too much of a child to understand," Yseult said coldly. "Pictures like that ought to be at the disposal of everyone and it's impossible to see them properly, even though so many of them are lighted."

"I may be younger than you," Len retorted hotly, "but at least I'm old enough to know that doing what you suggest would be stealing from God! They were painted for Him and they ought to remain where they are."

The mistresses were busy answering questions from the others, but Mary-Lou, who had, as her juniors often complained bitterly, ears that could hear the grass growing caught part of this. "What are you two arguing about?" she asked quickly, coming to them.

"Yseult wants to *steal* the cathedral pictures and put them in a picture gallery!" Len said. "She says I'm too young to understand, but I do know that it would be stealing all right! They were given to God."

Yseult's face flamed at this blunt speaking. "There's no question of stealing in it," she said heatedly. "But that's what comes of taking children like Len to see such things."

Mary-Lou stopped her at once. Len's eyes were flashing and she didn't want any kind of a scene in public between the pair. "I'm afraid Len is in the right, Yseult. What was given to God must remain His. And Yseult wasn't thinking of stealing, Len. That's quite the wrong way to put it. She only wanted those beautiful pictures to be put where they could be seen well. Only I do agree that to take pictures from a church and hang them in a secular place like a picture gallery is all wrong. Now come along, both of you! We're going to the Krone Hotel for Mittagessen and we don't want to be late or we'll throw out all their arrangements and then they won't love us. There's Rosamund looking for you, Len. Hop off and join her. Come along with me, Yseult. Have you ever been abroad before?"

Len knew better than to disobey Mary-Lou, so she ran off to join Rosamund and the rest of her particular clan who were waving impatiently at her. Mary-Lou joined up with Yseult who was looking sulky, and they descended the steps together.

"Why did you back up Len?" she suddenly burst out. "It's a lot of nonsense, all that about pictures being in church. They ought to be in art galleries——"

"Well, that's one point of view," Mary-Lou broke in. "But it certainly isn't everyone's. Come off it, Yseult! Pictures painted especially for a church belong to that church. How would you like it if someone walked into your home and snaffled all the best of *your* pictures and carted them off to the nearest art gallery? It's precisely the same principle."

Yseult could not see it, however, and she stalked along at Mary-Lou's side with her nose in the air.

At the foot of the steps, they were told to get into their groups again and go quietly down the Kronen Gasse to the Krone Hotel where their meal would be awaiting them.

"What a quiet sort of place this is," Hilary remarked to Mary-Lou, having joined her and Yseult. "It seems almost asleep. It's only a little after midday and yet there aren't a lot of people about and the shops seem to be quiet."

"Perhaps everyone's having Mittagessen," Mary-Lou suggested.

Jo Scott, who was walking with Heather Clayton just in front of them, looked back. "It reminds me a little of Fribourg," she said. "You get the same peaceful kind of atmosphere there."

"It reminds me a lot of Berne," Hilary responded. "Look at those old gabled houses over there. That's the sort of thing you see in Berne."

"And it has heaps of fountains like Berne, too," Heather agreed.

"I'd like to spend a weekend here," Hilary said. "I think it would be a real rest."

"So would I," Mary-Lou returned. "Hello! Here we are! Now we'll have to wait for the rest. Hi, Emerence! Off the road! I know this is a quiet place but that doesn't mean that you kids can go dickey-dancing all over the road regardless! We don't want to have to go back and break the news to Miss Annersley that we've left you on the road as strawberry jam!"

Emerence hopped back on to the pavement with a broad grin. "What a really nasty thing to say!" she retorted. "O.K. I'll stay put. Anyhow, here come Willy and Ferry, so we'll have Mittagessen in a few minutes, thank goodness!"

"Really, Emerence! How can you be so greedy?" Yseult took it on herself to say.

Emerence chuckled. "Not greedy—hungry! After all that art and architecture I guess I could eat an elephant!" She eyed Yseult with dislike before she added, "But I suppose *you* will require only a little soup and an ice. Or didn't they *have* ices in the days of King Arthur?"

"Be quiet!" Hilary said firmly. "Don't answer her, Yseult. Anyhow, you can't," she added with relief in her tones as the two mistresses reached them. "Do we go straight in, Miss Ferrars?"

"Yes—through those doors and straight on to the Speisesaal. Our tables have been booked and the Kellner will show you where to go," Miss Ferrars replied.

They went in quietly and very demurely and were speedily seated round the two tables provided for them at one end of the big Speisesaal. Soup was brought, hot and savoury, and was followed by fried lake trout. This was served with roast potatoes seasoned with herbs and flavoured with something no one could name, but definitely delicious. For a sweet, they had a choice between japonnais and millefeuilles and it is on record that Emerence made away with three helpings of the latter!

"Where do we go now?" Hilary asked when they were out in the street again, all with freshly washed hands and faces and hair redone so that they looked very trim.

"To the arsenal!" Miss Ferrars said promptly; and she

looked at Miss Wilmot and the pair of them giggled as if they were no older than their charges.

"Why is it so funny?" Len asked with a puzzled air.

"Oh, you'll see when you get there," Miss Wilmot told her quickly. "Come along, girls! We can't waste time, standing about. Come along! We'll see the Rathaus as we go and, with luck, we may get there in time for you to see the procession when the clock chimes the hour. But you'll have to hurry."

Only Yseult, who thought this sort of amusement beneath her dignity, was prepared to loiter after that. They lined up and scurried along the quiet streets—quieter than ever just now when most folk were at home or in a restaurant, busy with the midday meal. They reached the Marktplatz at one corner of which stands the lovely Rathaus, and lingered to admire the fountain and the seventeenth century statue of St Ursus before they reached the clock just before it struck two, and were delighted with the procession of mechanical figures. Then the two mistresses hurried them on, along the Barfüsser Gasse and they reached the arsenal.

"What a great, enormous place!" Rosamund cried as they stood gazing at the massive building which houses the most important collection of armour and weapons in Switzerland. "The Swiss must think an awful lot of that sort of thing."

"Of course they do! Don't forget the Swiss Guard who died to a man on the stairs when the Paris mob came to grab poor old Louis XVI and Marie Antoinette," Mary-Lou said. "And they still have the Swiss Guard at the Vatican. And for centuries one of the ways in which the Government collected money for their expenses was by hiring their men-at-arms to anyone who would pay heavily enough."

"They didn't!" Eve exclaimed.

"Didn't they just! Haven't you ever heard of the Swiss mercenaries in history?" Hilary backed her friend up.

"Oh! Is *that* what they were? I didn't know. But did

155

the people like it? Why did they put up with it? What about all the wives and mothers?"

"They hadn't any say-so. They just *had* to put up with it," Mary-Lou explained.

"It's no worse than the conscription you get in most countries," Hilary added. "Except, of course, that the men's services aren't sold to anyone. They serve for their own countries. And those who came through and were lucky often collected a fair amount of loot as well."

"I see." But Eve spoke very doubtfully. Then the mistresses called them to order and, lining up, they marched in.

It was just as well that neither Miss Ferrars nor Miss Wilmot had allowed much lingering, for the girls found plenty to interest them, including an executioner's sword with more than a hundred notches on its edge; four hundred suits of armour of all periods, some of them simply magnificent with inlays of bronze, silver and even gold and all gleaming with polish and hard rubbing; and the Orgeleschutz, a forerunner of the machine gun, with about thirty small barrels fixed in a triangular framework which was swung on a pivot. The courteous guide who took them round explained that thirteen shots could be fired by a single charge. Then the thing was swung round to discharge another thirteen and the final four came on the third side.

"When was it invented?" Emerence asked in rather awed tones.

"About 1550," he replied. "I imagine it was felt to be a marvel of invention in those days and I sometimes wonder what the inventors would have said to present-day guns that can fire hundreds of rounds in one long stream."

They saw the gorgeous tapestry tent captured from Charles the Bold of Burgundy at Morat in 1476, and also his own shield. Jo Scott looked at them thoughtfully. Then she turned to Nancy Wilmot.

"Morat," she said. "Wasn't that the battle that the great lime tree at Fribourg came from? The one that grew from a twig in the hat of a young soldier who dashed home to tell the people of Charles's defeat and died as soon as he had gasped out the news? I remember we saw in the summer before last when we were there."

"Quite right," the mistress said briskly.

"I remember that, too," Mary-Lou remarked. "And also that the slaughter of the Burgundians was so awful that Lake Morat ran red with blood and to this day when red water-lilies appear on it, they are called Burgundian Blood."

After that, they went up to the top rooms in the building where one of the first things they saw was a life-size model of a Swiss mercenary of 1754. The guide told them that at one time, when the door was opened, the figure saluted.

"But one day a timid old lady came—but very timid," he said with twinkling eyes. "When she saw this figure salute, she fainted and had to be carried downstairs. So then it was decided to disconnect the electrical wires that worked it and now it is as you see it—quite still."

"Oh, hard luck!" Margot cried. "I'd have loved to see it salute!"

"But, alas, it is still disconnected," he replied.

They enjoyed going round these rooms, too. But when he left them to roam about by themselves, they discovered a practical joke which the Solothurnians had left.

Among the armour captured at Morat was that belonging to the Duke of Burgundy's jester. Len and Co. crowded round it admiringly. It was made for a dwarf and was jet-black over a doublet of coloured silk. The headpiece in particular took their fancy. It has a grotesque upturned snout painted a brilliant red and an open mouth beneath, also red.

"How frightfully funny!" Len exclaimed. She put out her hand and took hold of the snout. "His nose couldn't be there, sure——"

She got no further. As she gripped it, she had raised the visor and a jet of water struck her well and truly from the mouth.

Len gasped and the others exploded with laughter.

"Ow!" cried Len. "My coat's all wet!"

Jo produced her handkerchief. "Keep still and I'll dry

you down. But what a joke!" She paused in her rubbing to look round them with dancing eyes. "It's a pity we should keep this to ourselves. We really ought to share it with the others!"

"So we ought!" Margot's blue eyes were one wicked twinkle. "I wonder if Willy and Ferry know about it?"

"I'll bet they do!" Emerence said with deep conviction. "Don't you remember how they giggled? We can't work it on them, but we could on some of the rest."

"O.K. The first to come," Jo decided, standing up. "There, Len! It's only clean water and most of it's off. Now who's coming?"

It proved to be Mary-Lou, Hilary and Yseult, who had tacked on to them.

"What have you got there?" Mary-Lou asked, coming to see what was interesting them. "Oh, I say! That's rather nifty, isn't it? But what a tiny affair! It must have been made for a dwarf! What does the note say?" She read it aloud. "Yes; I believe jesters were often deformed," she added. "Goodness! What a snout the poor soul must have had!"

"Cocked heavenwards!" Hilary said. "How about that, Yseult? Not much like what's-her-name's, is it? You know the one, don't you?"

"Do you mean *Lynette*?" Yseult asked in superior tones. "Hers was 'tip-tilted like the petal of a flower', as Tennyson says."

"That's the woman! Not much flowerlike about that!"

"Jesters were often grotesquely ugly," Yseult informed them. "This poor man no doubt was chosen because he *was* a dwarf and had just such a nose——"

She had laid her hand on the snout and drawn it over the curve as she spoke. Now she held the tip and inadvertently raised it. At once the jet flew forth and hit her squarely and her companions all went off into fits of laughter which were redoubled at the sight of her disgusted face.

"Oh!" she cried. "How stupid! What absurd nonsense! And to find it in a museum of all places! Really, I do think people are ridiculous! There's nothing *funny* about it and I don't see why you are all giggling in that childish way!" And she glared round at them, completing their loss of self-control.

"*Ah!*" said a pleased voice behind them. "So you've found the dwarf's armour! Anyone tried to raise the visor?"

It was Miss Wilmot who had come ahead while Miss Ferrars discussed a point of interest with the rest further behind. Giggles greeted her question.

"I did," Len said. "And Yseult has just done it." She chuckled and added, "Did you, Miss Wilmot?"

"I did—and got a showerbath. Keep it dark you people and we'll see if we can work it off on someone else!" Nancy Wilmot had always been full of fun and she turned to Yseult. "Wipe your coat quickly before they come, Yseult. Good gracious!" as the girl's expression struck her. "Can't you take a joke? Trot her off, Hilary and Mary-Lou, and dry her down. Here come the rest!"

Yseult hardly cared to make a fuss after Miss Wilmot's surprised query, so she let the two prefects draw her away to a corner where they wiped her down while Miss Ferrars appeared with the others thronging round her.

"Oh, what a *sweet* little suit of armour!" Caroline Sanders exclaimed in sentimental tones when she saw the figure. "It must have been made for a little boy."

"No; for the Duke's jester," Con Maynard said sweetly. "Hadn't he a funny headpiece. And just lift it and look inside, Caroline!"

All unsuspecting, Caroline came to stand in front of the figure and lift the visor and the joke came off once more, while everyone else roared with laughter. The jet was not enough to drench anyone and it was, as Jo had said, clean water. She shrieked with surprise; but then she laughed, too, as she shook herself dog-fashion.

"Oh, what a yell! And the *last* thing you'd expect in a place like this! Who else was caught?"

"Me—and Yseult," Len said cheerfully.

"Oh, I *wish* I'd seen it!" Caroline said yearningly.

"Then you wouldn't have been caught," Jo pointed out.

"Well, if you've quite finished amusing yourselves with it, shall we go and see what else we can find?" Miss Ferrars asked blandly. "Time's flying and we want to have Kaffee und Kuchen here and we must meet the coach on time. Come along, all of you!"

She led them off and after a tour of the quiet streets where they admired the beautiful old houses and did a little shopping, they went into a restaurant where they had their coffee accompanied by the kinds of pastries that only the Swiss know how to produce. It was while they were enjoying themselves, that Con Maynard made a suggestion which was taken up with acclamation.

"Couldn't we buy some cakes and take them home for the rest to have tomorrow? I'll give fifty centimes."

"So'll I!" Len cried. "Jo, what about you?"

One by one they handed over their offerings and, with some addition from the mistresses and prefects, they found they had enough to take home a great box of Leckerli which would rejoice the hearts of everyone.

"That was a good idea, Con," Miss Ferrars said as, the visit ended, they clambered into the waiting coach.

"Yes; it was," Len agreed. "And I've got another. I'm going to coax Mamma to bring us here during the hols and then we'll persuade her to lift that dwarf's visor and won't she yell!"

"You wicked imp!" Miss Wilmot said. "Do you really think she'll fall for it? How do you know one of us won't tell her first?"

"Because you never spoil sport," Len said simply.

And after that, there was no more to be said.

CHAPTER FIFTEEN

ENTER—AN OLD ACQUAINTANCE!

"BITTE, mein Fräulein, a lady would speak with you."

Miss Annersley looked up from the form lists she was studying with a concentrated frown. "Did she give you her name, Gretel?"

"Ja, mein Fräulein. She says she is Mees Bubb."

The Head's eyebrows climbed upwards to her hair, but she merely said, "Thank you, Gretel. Did you show her into the Saal?"

"Ja, mein Fräulein." Gretel curtsied and left the room and Miss Annersley, after a quick glance at her fingers to make sure that her fountain-pen had *not* leaked over them as it had a habit of doing at the most crucial moments, pushed her lists into a drawer and then, making sure that she was otherwise as trig and trim as a head mistress ought to be, swept out and along to the Saal.

A tall, broadly built woman in a well-worn tweed coat rose at her entrance. Under her hat, her hair was cropped and grey. Her face was aquiline and distinctly hard in expression and she had an air of decision to which her voice added, for it was keen and incisive, pitched rather high and with a metallic ring which was in direct contrast to Miss Annersley's.

"Miss Bubb, I think?" the Head said, offering her hand.

The visitor gripped it firmly and shook it equally firmly. "Yes," she said. "We have never met before, but at one time I stood in your place *pro tem*. You were in hospital, suffering from the effects of a bad motoring accident, I believe. I am glad to see that you appear to have recovered completely."

Miss Annersley waved her to a seat and took another herself. "Do sit down. Yes; I was *hors de combat* for a year, but after that I had fully recovered, I am thankful to say. In fact, we all did."

"Excellent! I remember at the time I was at the Chalet School they were all very anxious about you. That was the time, too, when one of Lady Russell's little girls had also had an accident. I trust she is recovered, too?"

"Oh yes. Josette is here with us. But," Miss Annersley added with a sudden flashing smile. "I'm sure you wouldn't recognise her now. She is a big, sturdy girl, as strong and healthy as possible. They were out in Canada for a couple of years and though Josette had really recovered before that, she still had a frail look. Canada put paid to that, though. At sixteen, Josette is one of the healthiest creatures imaginable."

"There was another girl, I remember—a pretty, feather-headed child."

"Oh, Sybil is one of our best prefects these days. She has grown into a very lovely girl and a very trustworthy one, too."

"Indeed?" Miss Bubb paused. Then she said, "You know, I had no idea the school had moved here. In fact I thought you were still in Armishire."

"Oh, no. We left Plas Howell some years ago—nearly six, to be exact. We were for some time at the Big House on St Briavel's, a little islet off the south coast of Wales. Then it was decided to open a new branch of the Sanatorium up here and so we brought a good part of the school as well. We had always hoped to return to the Alps as soon as possible, you know. This is our third year up here."

"Really? I had no idea of that."

There was another pause, during which the Head remained sitting easily in her armchair while Miss Bubb was evidently revolving some question in her mind. Having no notion what she could want, Miss Annersley kept silence. Presently, the visitor broached the real reason for her call.

"It was only last Sunday that I heard from a lady at present living at the Rösleinalp that the Chalet School was up here. She told me her daughter and step-daughter were both members—a Mrs Carey."

"Yes; Mary-Lou Trelawney is another of our prefects. And Verity Carey is a member of Va. They are both charming girls. Mrs Carey and her husband have been at the Rösleinalp for more than a year now. She was very ill with bronchial pneumonia and as her chest has always been delicate, the doctors advised a lengthy visit in high mountain air. He was seriously injured during the Murray-Cameron Expedition and has never been really well since. However, this sojourn has done them both all the good in the world and they are hoping to return home when the summer comes."

"Yes, so she gave me to understand." But Miss Bubb did not seem to be very interested in the Careys and the Head wondered anew why she had come at all.

"I don't know if you remember any of our mistresses," she began. "Let me see. Several of those at the school when you were in charge have left, of course. Miss Linton is married and so is Miss Burnett, though our P.T. mistress is a younger sister of hers. Miss Slater is head of the mathematical department of a very big day-school near London and Mme de Bersac and her husband are living in the old family home in France. She has three children now. Thérèse, better know to us as Tessa, is at school here. The other two, Pierre and Jean are just babies still. But we have Mlle Berné who is at St Mildred's, our finishing branch; and Matron Gould is still with us. Miss Phipps who had charge of the Kindergarten is keeping house for a brother on the Darling Downs and Miss Cochrane has given up teaching and is in partnership with another Old Girl of ours. They run a music shop in Auckland, New Zealand and, I believe are making quite a good thing of it." She paused to smile and went on. "And of course, you met my co-Head, Miss Wilson. She also is at St. Mildred's, though we see a good deal of her here," she added.

"I remember Miss Wilson," Miss Bubb said abruptly. "It was owing to her return that I was able to resign the post so quickly."

"I wish she'd get on with it!" Miss Annersley thought impatiently. "This isn't a mere social call—I can see that. What on earth *does* she want?"

Miss Bubb also seemed to feel that it was time she came to the point. She cleared her throat and said, "Well, I must explain why I'm here. The fact of the matter is that I'm rather at a loose end just now. I had better explain that after leaving the Chalet School, I went into partnership with a friend in another school. Unfortunately, we found it impossible to agree on certain points so we dissolved the partnership. Since then I have had one or two financial losses."

"Oh, I'm sorry to hear that!" Miss Annersley exclaimed, real sympathy in her voice.

"Thank you. It was also unfortunate that I had a very bad attack of influenza in the early autumn which left me very shaky. My doctor advised me to come out to Switzerland for some months and avoid the English winter. I took his advice and feel much better in consequence. Unluckily, I find that my funds will not stand this much longer. Having heard that you were here, I wondered if you could give me a post as part-time mistress. I took Honours in Classics at Cambridge and I think I may say without conceit that I have always been a successful coach. I can, of course, give you plenty of testimonials, but the fact that at one time I was acting Head of the Chalet School seems to me to be sufficient testimonial." She stopped suddenly and then went on in rather different tones, "I should be really very glad if you could employ me, as I feel I ought to stay in this atmosphere some months longer if it is at all possible."

Miss Annersley was thinking swiftly. Nothing she had ever heard of the lady made her at all anxious to employ her. Still, on the momentous occasion to which she had alluded, she had been in full charge and the quarrel between her and the school over various methods she had seen fit to try to introduce without any reference to anyone else, could not be begun again in present circumstances. Also it must be admitted that Miss Annersley was a soft-hearted creature and now that she looked more closely at her visitor, she saw distinct signs of wear and tear.

"I can't give you any definite answer now," she said finally. "I must consult Miss Wilson first. As I told you, she and I are co-Heads and I could hardly make such a decision without discussing it with her first. So far as Lady Russell is concerned, I have full power to engage any member of staff I choose, so I need not wait for her. Are you still at the Rösleinalp?"

"Oh, yes; I expect to stay there for another fortnight at least."

"I see. You are at the Gasthaus, I suppose?"

"Er—no. In present circumstances I can't afford their terms. I have a room in one of the chalets near by and find my own food—except for breakfast."

"I see. Well, if you will give me your address, I'll talk it over with Miss Wilson and also Mrs Maynard——"

"Is she up here, too?" Miss Bubb interrupted her.

"Yes; her husband is head of the Sanatorium up here. They live at Freudesheim—that tall house round the bend. Her triplet daughters—did you ever meet them?—are at school, of course. Leading lights of our Inter V, I may say. The two elder boys are at prep school in England."

"Two elder boys? She had only one when I was at Plas Howell."

Miss Annersley laughed. "Oh, but she's gone on since then. Besides those five, there are Michael who spends the term down at Montreux with friends who have boys of the same age, so he shares their tutor. The twins who come next are three years younger and no companions for him. Mike is much better with the Emburys when Steve and Charles are away."

"Did you say *twins* as well?" Miss Bubb exclaimed. "But that makes *eight*!"

"Nine—baby Cecil will be a year old on April 2nd," the Head returned, smiling. "She was a great joy when she arrived. Mrs Maynard has four boys and five girls."

"Good Heavens!" Miss Bubb looked utterly startled.

The school bell rang and Miss Bubb stood up. "I mustn't keep you. I expect you have a lesson now. But you will think over my request? And I hope you will feel that you can give me a favourable answer."

Before Miss Annersley could reply, the door opened and Miss Wilson walked in. "Hilda! Do you know where that parcel of chemicals I asked Rosalie to order for me has been put?" she demanded. Then she saw the visitor who had been sitting in the well of the room and apologised promptly. "I beg your pardon. I didn't know you were engaged. I'll go and find Rosalie."

"Come in," Miss Annersley said with a smile. "Can you recognise an old acquaintance, Nell?"

Miss Bubb turned round and Miss Wilson gave an exclamation. "Why, Miss Bubb! I *thought* it was you who went past our gate the other night."

"Was that you, Miss Wilson? I did not recognise you. I should not have done so now if I had not guessed who you must be. You look very much better and, if I may say so, very much younger than you did in the days when I was at the Chalet School before. You must have mended well?"

"Oh, yes; I mended very well," Miss Wilson said cheerfully. "I'm afraid I can't be so complimentary to you. You don't look very fit."

"Miss Bubb has had a very nasty illness, but she is much better now," Miss Annersley said. "She is up at the Rösleinalp just now. As for your chemicals, I believe you'll find them in the stock room. Rosalie is down in Interlaken, seeking some fresh supplies so you won't find her here."

"I see. Thanks! I'll just go and rescue my belongings and then I must fly. Va are waiting for me. Good afternoon, Miss Bubb. What fun to meet again after all these years!" Miss Wilson nodded at Miss Bubb and vanished.

Miss Annersley turned to her visitor. "I'll certainly talk over your proposal with Miss Wilson and I'll let you know as soon as possible. May I have the address?"

Miss Bubb gave her a card. "It's written down. I couldn't be sure I should see you." She turned to go. Then she turned back. "I—I hope it will be a *favourable* answer. I—I really do need the employment."

"I will let you know as soon as possible," Miss Annersley replied. She felt that she must not raise any hopes until she had gone into the matter with Miss Wilson.

Miss Bubb nodded. "Thank you. Good afternoon, Miss Annersley."

When she had finally gone, Miss Annersley turned from the door to find her co-Head waiting for her with a boding look.

"And what's the why of all this, Hilda? What set the woman to come here?"

"I'll tell you all about it if you'll come for after-dinner

coffee this evening," Miss Annersley retorted. "I'm due for a session with VIb and goodness only knows what Va are doing while they're waiting for you!"

"Oh, I'd forgotten them! Very well; I'll be along between twenty and half-past; and remember! I shall expect to hear all!" Miss Wilson said as she made off in the direction of the stock room to hunt up her missing supplies.

Miss Wilson duly arrived that evening after Abendessen, and was met in the drive by Joey Maynard who greeted her cheerfully with, "Hello, Nell! What's at the bottom of Hilda's sudden message?"

"Something, I don't doubt. For one thing, an old acquaintance of yours turned up today. It's something to do with that."

"An old acquaintance? Who?"

"Oh, a *dear* friend of yours!" Nell Wilson cooed.

Joey gave her a quick look. "H'm! Something odd here! What's behind it all?"

"You'll hear in a moment. But of course Hilda *would* send for you, seeing you were in the thick of things at the time. All right, Joey. I haven't suddenly taken leave of my senses as I can see you're wondering. Come along in and leave your shawl. But I do wonder," she added, half to herself, "what exactly Hilda is after."

They deposited their wraps on the big settle in the entrance hall and then turned across it and down the short corridor which led to the Head's private wing. Miss Annersley was waiting for them in her own pretty drawing-room. With her were Matron, Mlle de Lachennais, Mlle Berné, Frau Mieders and Miss Denny, whose brother was recovering again so that his sister was free to give her time to the school. Rosalie Dene was seated at the coffee table, engaged in dispensing coffee, and the Head herself was handing cream cakes.

"Come along, you two!" she cried as the pair entered. "You're the last. Cecil all right, Joey?"

"Fit as a fiddle. Rösli is sitting in my bedroom with her endless knitting, ready to fly if any of the babies so much

167

as whimpers, so I'm free for the moment. What's all this in aid of, Hilda?"

"You'll hear in a moment. Go and get your coffee from Rosalie and find seats somewhere, you two. Then we can begin."

They did as she told them and when everyone was sitting with coffee and cream cakes, Miss Annersley also sat down and came straight to the point.

"I know you're all wondering why I've convened this meeting. I had a visitor this morning whom you all know —Miss Bubb."

"Miss *Bubb*!" It came as a chorus, but Joey's voice rang above the others.

"What on earth is *she* doing here?" she added.

"Staying up at the Rösleinalp. What's wrong with that? We haven't bought up the whole of Switzerland, you know."

Joey made a face at her. "We have not, but I'd just as soon not have *that* woman within twenty miles of me! I loathed her with a deep and deadly loathing. What did she want, anyhow?"

"To ask if we could give her some part-time teaching."

"I hope you told her the answer was in the negative," Rosalie Dene said.

"I didn't. I told her I must consult Nell first. When I came to think it over, I decided that the rest of you ought also have some say in the matter. *You* had to deal with her at the time. I never saw her before in my life."

"Well, you ought to have told her that we didn't require her services, thank you," Joey said with emphasis.

"Did she give any reason *why* she should apply to us, of all people, for a job? I shouldn't have thought she'd have had the cheek after all that happened then. What years ago it is!" she added. "Steve was just a baby of a few months old. Oh, by the way, Hilda, was *I* mentioned by any chance? And did you tell her about my lengthy family?"

"Yes, to both questions," Miss Annersley replied sweetly.

"She called you 'a somewhat self-assured young woman',

I remember," Miss Wilson said reminiscently. "I don't think she exactly cottoned to you, Joey."

"It was mutual! I certainly didn't cotton to *her*! But Hilda! I seem to remember that she went into partnership with someone in another school. What's happened to it?"

"It didn't work and the partnership was dissolved. Now stop talking, all of you, and let me tell you exactly why she came to us. You can't understand till you know." And having secured silence, Miss Annersley told the story Miss Bubb had given her.

"I—see!" Miss Wilson looked thoughtful. "What do you want us to do about it?"

"Not have her here again, I hope!" Rosalie Dene sat upright. "I never want to see the woman again! She seemed to think that a school secretary was on a par with a galley slave! Never once, all the time she was with us, did I finish work before eight o'clock—except on Saturdays and Sundays. If Madge hadn't been so anxious about Josette at the time, I'd have handed in my resignation to take effect at once!"

"I tried to do much the same thing," Joey said. "Only I'd sent for Nell and she came in answer to my shrieks for help and accused me of trying to let her down. I couldn't do a thing about it after that."

"This is news to me!" Miss Annersley sat up and looked round them.

"My dear, you were so ill at the time that no one told you anything. When you finally came back to us, it was more than a year past and we were more or less forgetting about it," Nell Wilson told her. "I did give you a brief outline, but I saw no reason to fill in details. It would have been enough to give you a bad relapse."

Mlle Berné looked up. "Me, I did not like her, though she interfered very little with me. Has she been as ill as she said, Hilda, do you think?"

"I should say she had been seriously ill," Hilda Annersley replied slowly. "It was in September and she still had that bleached look one expects after serious illness. Also, I should say she hadn't exaggerated about her financial losses. She looked very shabby and she told me quite frankly that she was unable to afford the Gasthaus terms and was living in one of the chalets and eating out."

There was a little pause. Then Hilda Annersley set down her cup and leaned forward. "I don't say I *want* her here. But do remember this, you people. If she comes as a part-time mistress, the conditions will be very different. She will be here perhaps two days a week to take the very advanced Latin—and you know, Julie, that you told me that you were finding it difficult to fit in all the work you wanted to do."

Mlle de Lachennais spoke. "She would not be living here?"

"In the school, do you mean? Certainly not! We have no room as it is. In fact, the celebrations apart, I have refused to take any new pupils for that very reason. The Dawbarns, Doris Hill, Primrose Trevoase and Gwen Jones are all coming next term and that makes us full up. And they aren't new girls at all."

"Quite right!" Matron said. "All I hope is that the Dawbarns and Primrose have had time to reform during the past two or three years. As you always used to say, Joey, the Dawbarns were born to be hanged; and Primrose was quite as bad."

Miss Annersley laughed. "Matey, have you forgotten that every one of them is at least fifteen now? Doris and Gwen are the same age as Mary-Lou and Co. and, in any case, were a law-abiding pair."

"What are we going to do when the Christmas term comes?" Joey asked.

Miss Wilson waved her down. "No, you *don't*!" Then, as Joey gaped at her, "I mean we're having no side-tracking. I know your gifts that way of old and you aren't exhibiting them at this present moment. We've got to decide what we're going to do about Miss Bubb—drat the woman! Why must she come and disturb our peaceful community in this way? Well, Hilda, I can see that, as usual, you're inclined to be soft-hearted. I suppose you want us to give her a hand?"

"You must do as you think right," Miss Annersley said.

"I loathed the woman when she was with us before. Still, as you say, the conditions will be quite different this time. And we really do need someone to help with the Latin and Greek."

"Oh, well, I needn't have anything to do with the staff room on her days," Rosalie said uncharitably. "I'm sorry, Hilda. I see your point and I suppose we ought to help her; but that doesn't make me any more inclined to love her."

Miss Annersley turned to the two who, so far, had not spoken. "Sarah and Anna, what do *you* say?"

Miss Denny shook her head. "It's nothing to do with me. I never had anything to do with her."

"And you, Anna?"

"Oh, I will agree. She did not interfere with my work. I did not like her, but if she is poor and in need and has asked us for help, we must help."

"Well, all I can say is that I hope her misfortunes have softened her!" Joey said piously. "All right Hilda. You tell her she has a job so far as I'm concerned. As you say, she can hardly interfere with the way the school is run."

"And you, Nell? I can't do it if you don't agree."

"You haven't given me much option, have you?" Miss Wilson spoke ruefully. "I'll agree. She can still live up at the Rösleinalp and come down twice in the week for work. I'll agree to that. The only thing I won't countenance is having her living among us."

"As I told you, there won't be any room. If she finds the Rösleinalp too much of a strain, she can come to one of the chalets down here. But she can't live in the school. I doubt if she would like it herself. So that's settled. I'll write tomorrow and go and see her on Saturday when I'm going to spend the day with the Careys in any case. Thank you, everyone. And now, Rosalie, what about some more coffee? All our cups are empty. Has anyone decided what she's doing during the holidays? Jeanne, are you really going to Italy as you thought?"

The mistresses came for fresh coffee and, for the remainder of the session, other things were discussed.

CHAPTER SIXTEEN

THE term was beginning to fly. The weather prophets were proving themselves more accurate than usual and the long thaw which had set in at the beginning of March had continued. The streaks of green which had begun to appear on the Görnetz Platz were broadening each day and the last week of March saw the grass clear, though patches lingered in shadowy places. By April 1st, between the sun and a brisk wind, everywhere was drying up nicely.

Easter was late that year—almost as late as it could be. The school would break up on the Friday in Passion Week and return on the Thursday after Low Sunday. It made a very long Easter term, but that couldn't be helped. Then the Head announced at prayers on the Tuesday of that week that as they had been kept indoors so much during the early part of the term, it had been decided that for the last few days of term the morning, if fine, should be devoted to really long walks and any work would be done in the afternoons.

"Besides," she added, looking at them with laughing eyes, "we propose to institute a new event for the end of term. We owe the idea to Miss Ferrars who tells us that it was celebrated at her old school at the end of every term. We all like the idea so much, that we are adopting it forthwith. In future, fines paid for spills on the tablecloths are to go to provide funds for a Spot Supper at the end of term. We hold our first one on Thursday night."

There, she had to stop, for Emerence Hope had jumped to her feet and called for three cheers for Miss Ferrars which were given with a will, though Margot and Con pulled the instigator back on to her seat in a hurry.

The Head turned to laugh at her mistress before she turned back to lean forward on the lectern. "I have to break it to you that Spot Supper is also accompanied by

172

speeches," she said with mock solemnity. "Usually, these are made by any mistresses or girls new that term. As we had none this, we are calling on people who were new *last* term. I am giving you due warning so that you will have time to think out what you want to say. St Mildred's will join us for the event, of course, which means that all their new girls will make speeches, too. Miss Wilson is warning them today. We wind up with a sing-song and that, I hope, will send you home for the holidays ready to enjoy every moment of them.

"Now when I dismiss you, go to your splasheries and get ready for a walk. Then go out to your usual place and wait for your escort mistresses. And please don't forget that this is French day," she added. She nodded to Miss Lawrence who dashed into her march and the girls swung out briskly, every face beaming with delight at the thought of a long walk each morning till the end of term *and* the latest institution.

Miss Ferrars arrived to escort her own form. She told them to line up and when they had left the school gate behind, led them to the left.

"Where are we going, Miss Ferrars?" Jo Scott asked in very proper French.

"As far as St Lorenz and back. It'll give you a good stretch as it's four miles away, and put some good air into your lungs."

"Oh, que c'est merveilleux!" Len Maynard cried with her frenchiest manner. "J'aime beaucoup St Lorenz!"

Shepherded by Miss Ferrars, they stepped out at a brisk pace. It was a beautiful morning, bright and sunny, with a blue sky across which the piled white clouds were racing before the fresh breeze. It was so fine that Matron had agreed to the discarding of scarves and they were in walking shoes which was a delightful change after all these weeks of boots. As they reached the gate of Freudesheim, Joey Maynard appeared, pushing the pram in which her youngest daughter was sitting upright, gurgling away, while the silvery-fair twins, Felix and Felicity, ran on ahead, shouting with delight. The girls had to stop and speak to

173

Cecil of course, and Joey had a few remarks to make to them.

"I've just heard about your Spot Supper and I'm coming to it," she announced just before she called the twins in and parted from Inter V.

"You?" Jo Scott cried. "But you aren't a Chalet girl now, Godmother!"

"Am I not? I'll thank you to remember, young woman, that I'm the oldest Old Girl there is. I was a pupil of the Chalet School before ever it came into existence! So put *that* on your needles and knit it!" With which valediction, she wheeled off the baby, leaving them all laughing at her very Irish speech.

"Come along!" Miss Ferrars commanded. "We'll never get to St Lorenz at this rate!"

They set off again, walking in line until they were quite clear of the Platz. Then when they had turned the curve of the great motor road, Miss Ferrars gave the word to break ranks and was at once besieged by a small mob.

"Tell us about Spot Supper, Miss Ferrars," Margot Maynard coaxed. "What did you do?"

"Well, you all know I went to a day school, don't you? It was eight miles from my home which meant having school lunch. We were fined a ha'penny for every splash we made on the cloth and with those fines, Spot Supper was provided."

"You must have been splashy!" Len giggled.

"My dear girl, there were well over a hundred of us and some of the younger girls were apt to be terribly messy—at first!"

"You can't always *help* splashing," Emerence remarked gloomily. She had been mulcted of seven centimes during the past two days for that very thing.

"No; but you can be careful," her form mistress told her. "Well, we all used to stay at the school for tea. We met in the gym at six and, at half-past, we lined up and marched into the dining room and round the tables, singing the Spot Supper song."

"What was it?" Charmian demanded. "Can *we* use it?"

"Certainly not! It belongs to St Mary's High. But we are going to have one of our own, to the tune of *John Brown's Body* which you all know. You're having the words dictated to you this afternoon first thing so that you can all learn them by heart."

"Oh, good!" came an enthralled chorus.

"What did you have to eat—anything special?" Heather looked expectant.

"It was always the same. We began with sausages and mashed potato, followed by creams and jellies and fruit. We had lemonade to drink with it. At Christmas, we had mincepies; a special cake at Easter; ices in the summer. The Head gave those."

"And what about the speeches?" Rosamund queried.

"Oh, they came at the end of supper." Kathie stopped to laugh and the girls looked eager.

"Who made the first one?" Con wanted to know.

"The Head, always. When we had finished and the tables had been cleared, we all drummed on them with our fists while the Head Girl called for the Head. Then we joined in and shouted 'Spee—eech—spee—eech!' until she stood up. We were quiet then, of course. After the Head, we did the same thing with any new mistresses and after them, the new girls, beginning with the topmost form. Then we all stood up and marched round the room, singing the song again and so out to the gym. There were chairs for the staff and we girls sat on the floor and we sang all our favourite songs until eight o'clock when we went home. It was good fun!"

"It sounds like it," Len said.

"Are we going to do all that?" Charmian inquired.

"We are—Girls! Get to the side, quickly! Something's coming round the corner!"

The girls hurriedly scrambled to the sides of the road just in time as one of the Sanatorium's big ambulances came slowly past. When it had gone, they clustered round their mistress again, demanding to know what she had said in her first speech and if she meant to make a speech this time.

"As I'm the only new mistress last term—yes. But I propose you call on Mrs Maynard for one," Kathie said, her eyes brimful of mischief.

Joey's daughters shrieked with undutiful glee at the idea.

"We won't tell her a thing about it!" Margot exclaimed.

"No; we'll just all start pounding and calling for her," Len chuckled. "Won't she be mad, though!"

"*Can* we?" Betty asked. "After all, she's not exactly a *new* girl, is she?"

"Of course she isn't!" Con cried. "She really *is* the oldest Old Girl the school has. But I don't see that that need matter."

"She'll be coming as a visitor. *We* always called on visitors," Kathie told her.

"Then that will be four grown-ups," Joan Baker said thoughtfully.

"Four?" Again it was a chorus.

"Yes—Miss Annersley, Miss Wilson, Miss Ferrars and now Mrs Maynard."

"Yes; I'll be in good company," Kathie acknowledged.

Jo Scott had been thinking. "What about letting the rest know the procedure? I mean how the speeches should be started? They won't know, will they? Or are you going to tell them? We'll have to do something or if we start calling and thumping on our own the prefects will be sure to think we're only being noisy and interfere."

"That's why I've told you all this. You can tell all your own clan and they will join in. As for the prefects, I'm telling them myself."

"Oh, good!" they chorused. "Then *that'll* be all right!"

"And now, hadn't you better walk properly? We can't straggle across the road like this the whole way. We're making pests of ourselves to any motor traffic that may come along. Break up, girls!" She waved them off and they went, laughing and talking and, for a wonder, mostly contriving to remember that it was French day.

Len and Con remained with Miss Ferrars and pranced along beside her, asking questions about her school days and telling her a few of the less well-known legends of the school. Rosamund, Jo and Joan Baker had taken Yseult off with them and were doing their best to draw some sort of interest in the school's latest from her. Judging by the snatches she could hear of their chatter, they were finding it pretty stiff going and, not for the first time, Kathie felt a deep yearning to take her tiresome pupil by the shoulders and give her a good shaking.

They had just reached the shelf on which St Lorenz, the little village they were heading for, lay. It was quite small—a tiny whitewashed church with the usual onion bulb spire and about a score of little chalets and huts clustering round it. Kathie knew that the people worked hard all day. The children went to school in a larger village farther along the motor road and the men were cowherds, farmers and so on, doing wood carving in their spare time, while the women saw to the houses and did all the needle-work, laundering, and made lace or embroidery when they were at leisure.

Tethered to a stake at the entrance near the village, was a nanny-goat with two adorable kids skipping about near at hand while their mother kept an eye on them as she cropped the grass within reach of her tether—and the tether was unusually long.

The girls saw the babies. Some of them, having been warned many times to let goat-kids alone, especially if the goat was with them, contented themselves with admiration that was loud and vocal. But Yseult, born and brought up in a city, knew next to nothing about goats. Her eye fell on the babies and she made a dive for the nearest, exclaiming, "Oh, aren't you sweet!"

Master Billy was not accustomed to human beings who tried to pick him up with a wild swoop of long arms. He fled, maa-ing loudly, and the nanny goat lifted her head, saw her son threatened, put down her head and made a frantic dash at the great thing that had frightened her baby. The stake to which she had been tethered could not have been driven in far enough, for with the fury of her attack, she contrived to yank it out of the ground. Yseult realised the danger and turned and fled shrieking down the road, chased in grim earnest by the enraged mother.

Some of the girls turned and fled from the lady. Two or three of them, including the Maynards, tried to get hold of either the tether or the stake and pelted after the huntress. The frightened kids had scuttled to the far side of the shelf, voicing their woes in a series of high-pitched bleatings that brought everyone at home out of doors to see what was going on. Among them was a portly dame well into the sixties, who was the goat's owner. She gave an exclamation and bundled after her property as fast as her years and bulk would let her.

Meanwhile Len, famed among her own clan for her swiftness of foot, had contrived to grab the stake and was holding it firmly. Con reached her and added her strength and the goat was suddenly brought up short.

Yseult, still flying before the angry demon, glanced round, saw that the goat had stopped for a moment, took a wild leap to the side of the road and landed into a very healthy thorn bush, one of several which grew wild about the place. The yell she gave as she landed, outdid anything in that line she had so far achieved.

By this time, Miss Ferrars had also reached the stake and laid hold on it. The goat felt the check to her progress. She fought wildly and snapped the tether to the consternation of everyone. A raging goat is an unpleasant customer to meet when it is loose. She had lost sight of Yseult who was still entangled in the thorn bush and not ceasing to yell. But coming up quickly was a large figure bewailing the happening to her favourite. The goat was beyond all reason now. Her yellow eyes were flaming and it was clear that she meant to take it out of *somebody* for the fright she had had. She leaped round and headed for the valiant quartet which had collapsed in a heap on the ground when the tether snapped. Someone else loomed up and the goat made for her and butted well and truly. The next moment, she was lying under her owner's bulk, dazed and bruised and that stout lady was screaming even more loudly than Yseult who, by this time, was being released from her uncomfortable position by Rosamund and Jo who had rushed to the rescue. Some of the others were pulling Miss Ferrars and the Maynards back to their feet. Betty and Alicia had grabbed what was left of the tether and big Joan Baker and Heather Clayton were trying to heave the elderly lady to the upright. The rest of the dwellers in St Lorenz were coming up and two of the women came to the rescue of the goat's mistress and she was picked up and dusted down, what time the goat scrambled to her sharp little hoofs, glared round and began to try to limp away to where her kids had forgotten their fright and were playing again.

Betty and Alicia clung to the few feet of tether with all their might. Miss Ferrars having straightened her hat, came up with the stake and the other end, and then a car which had been running gently up the road slowed down at sight of the agitation. It stopped and the driver sprang out and came quickly to the rescue.

"What is wrong here?" he demanded. And the three Maynard girls shrieked delightedly, "Papa! The goat chased Yseult!"

"Oh, Father, do go and see the poor old lady. That bad goat butted her down!" This was Margot.

Con added her quota. "Oh, Papa! She fell right on top of the poor goat!"

Jack Maynard took it all in with one swift glance round and he gave a broad grin.

"Frau Huber's Hanni! She can be a raging fiend, that one! Bitte, meine Frau," he spoke courteously to the somewhat stunned lady, "has Hanni harmed you?"

"That devil of a goat!" Frau Huber cried, shaking her fist at the now subdued Hanni. "She would kill me—me, who feed her and deny myself all pleasures to give her the best of hay and oats during the winter! This is how she rewards me! To the butcher she shall go tomorrow!"

"Oh, no," the doctor said soothingly. "After all, she gives you butter and milk and cheese, meine Frau. When the little kids are grown, they will sell well. See; here comes Conrad. Conrad, come and attend to this imp of evil.

Tether her safely and make sure she can't pull out the stake again."

The big man who had come up, saluted and gave Frau Huber a grin. "I told you, my aunt, to leave Hanni and the kids in the shed till I could drive in the stake for you. She was well enough there for another morning. Now go home and make coffee and let the Herr Doktor see if she has harmed you. And what of the gracious young ladies?"

The "gracious young ladies" were standing round, nearly choking in their efforts to keep from laughing, now that the danger was over. Yseult had torn a stocking and lost her hair ribbon besides pricking her face and hands on the thorns, and Jo and Rosamund were also scratched. Miss Ferrars and the triplets were bruised—as Emerence said later, they had "gone with a whang!" No one else was hurt at all, except the goat who was very sore and stiff for the next two or three days. Even a goat can't receive a crashing weight of seventeen stone odd on top of her without suffering from it. As Jack Maynard said later when he had got the whole yarn, the wonder was that she had escaped without either a broken neck or broken ribs. In fact, he sent down to Interlaken for the vet to come and see to her, but that gentleman, reporting at Freudesheim later, said he could find nothing much wrong.

"All goats belong to the devil," he remarked as he left, "and *he* looks after his own!"

The women of St Lorenz insisted on giving everyone coffee or milk and Jack Maynard told Kathie to accept if she didn't want to insult them.

"Ask for milk, though," he advised her. "Their coffee is anything but nectar. Late for lessons? I'll go ahead in a moment and tell Hilda Annersley what's happened and not to expect any of you until she sees you. Meanwhile," with another broad grin, "it's been worth it to see that silly young ass Yseult forget her dignity for once and hear her laughing with the rest like a proper schoolgirl!"

This was true. Once she had got over her shock, Yseult had actually seen the funny side of the whole affair and as he spoke, she was giggling wholeheartedly in company with a bunch of her own form who, it may be remarked in passing, giggled at intervals the whole way home.

"All the same," Miss Annersley said pensively to Kathie when that young lady made her report in the study, "I *didn't* tell you to go headlong into an adventure. However, no one seems a penny the worse, so we'll let it go at that—except that your form can make a collection and present Frau Huber with a stout new tether for her goat. I don't suppose she has too much to come and go on, poor old soul. And certainly, if Yseult had not lost her head over a goat-kid, this would never have happened."

"No," Kathie agreed as she turned to go and make herself fit to be seen. "But if she hadn't, the chances are she'd never have forgotten how grown-up she is. The ice is broken now and I'm making it my business to see that it *stays* broken! I don't like grown-up schoolgirls!"

CHAPTER SEVENTEEN

THE FIRST "SPOT SUPPER"

THE prefects had taken good care to drag every iota of information about Spot Supper that they possibly could from Miss Ferrars. She had had to rack her memory for details until she was almost sorry she had described the event to some of her peers one wintry night when the Head had also been in the staff sitting room, thus starting a new tradition for the Chalet School. However, it was done now and, as she consoled herself by thinking, another term they would have it all at their finger-tips and not worry her any more. Besides, the Chalet School would certainly take their own way with it. And quite right, too!

As a result, when Thursday evening came, the girls all assembled in Hall, clad in their travelling frocks, since everything else was packed and the trunks had already gone off. When everyone was there, Elinor Pennell mounted the dais. "Now you all know what you have to do, don't you?" she began. "I take Miss Annersley and Julie Lucy, who is Head at St Mildred's, will take Miss Wilson. The other mistresses, including all the Matrons, Nurse, Miss Dene, and Miss Culver from St Mildred's, will come in with prefects or seniors. The rest of you pair off and line up after us. We all march *once* round Hall, singing the Spot Supper song, and then out and along to the Speisesaal where we march right round the tables. When you see us taking our seats, you all sit down—and remember, you younger folk, there's to be no scrum. You sit down on the first chair that comes your way. Or rather," for she knew her juniors, "you stand behind it until grace has been said. You can talk quietly until supper is over and in any language you like. When the tables have all been cleared, you come back to your seats and when I stand up, you can begin to drum and call on Miss Annersley for her speech. Miss Wilson comes next. Then Miss Ferrars and then Mrs Maynard. After that, we begin on the new girls. And I hope you've all got your speeches ready," she added severely.

"We've got them!" came in a chorus.

"Good! Then don't forget to stand up as soon as you're called on. After the speeches, we all line up again and go back to Hall, singing the Spot Supper song. You sit down near the dais—don't try to go down to the far end. You'll only be called up closer. Then we'll have sing-song till bedtime. That's all, I think. Now get ready for prayers. We're having them first tonight."

She jumped down and went to take her place among the prefects and the girls hurriedly opened their hymn books, while the Catholics marched out quietly to the gymnasium where their prayers would be held tonight as the Speisesaal was all ready for the supper.

As soon as prayers were over, the mistresses left the room. The Catholic girls marched in to join the rest and then the top doors at the end of Hall opened and the girls of St Mildred's appeared to be greeted joyfully.

"Be my partner, Betsy!" Barbara Chester called across to her cousin, Betsy Lucy.

Betsy nodded and laughed and came over to join her. Mary-Lou had lain claim to Katharine Gordon; and Rosamund, blushing furiously, had run to catch tall Hilary Wilson by the arm. In fact, as Lesley Malcolm, who had claimed Lala Winterton's sister, Polly, remarked, by the time they had finished, St Mildred's was well and truly mixed up with the rest of the school.

Then the mistresses from both branches arrived and were claimed by their partners. Miss Lawrence ran up to the piano to strike a chord, and the entire school set off on its long promenade, singing with gusto the words of the Spot Supper song which had been concocted by Miss Ferrars, Miss o'Ryan and Rosalie and went with a swing to the tune of *John Brown's Body*.

"Now the term is ended and our chores are fully
    done.
Many a tablecloth we've used and spots on every
    one!
Many a fine we've had to pay and now we have
    our fun—
        Spot Supper's on the way!
    Sing, sing, sing for our Spot Supper!
    Sing, sing, sing for our Spot Supper!
    Sing, sing, sing for our Spot Supper!
        Spot Supper's on the way!"

The gifted authoresses had refused to manage more than this. As Miss o'Ryan had pointed out, the girls could contribute further verses later, and one verse and a chorus was quite enough for a beginning!

By the time they had sung it five times, they were all in the Speisesaal, standing round the table, and Len giggled as she pointed out to Rosamund that everyone was well mixed-up for once. Only at the staff table were some of the mistresses, each with her attendant senior. The rest were anywhere!

Grace was said and they sat down. The tables were delightful with their pretty cloths, many-coloured glasses, and big dishes set down the full length, heaped with trifle, creams, jellies, honeycomb moulds, a delicious concoction of Karen's known to the girls as "Raspberry Fluff", méringues and plates of pastries peculiar to Switzerland. The staff had clubbed together and the result was piles of gay crackers between the eatables which added to the effect. And Mlle had spent her afternoon hanging Chinese lanterns over the electric bulbs to finish it off.

Then Karen and her satellites appeared bearing mighty trays on which were plates of steaming sausage and mash with her own special gravy as a finishing touch. Each tackled a table and when everyone had a plateful in front of her and before the maids could leave the room, Mary-Lou had leapt to her feet, crying, "Three cheers for Karen and Co.!"

The girls gave the cheers with a will, so Spot Supper got off to a good start, as Karen, beaming broadly on everyone, led the way back to the kitchen where a similar spread awaited the kitchen staff, complete, down to crackers.

A good many of the younger girls had abstained from eating at Kaffee und Kuchen and they were all hungry, so those platefuls disappeared in short order. The cakes came next and they had a choice of coffee or Karen's delicious fruit drinks. When all the food had vanished, they pulled crackers and found paper hats only. Miss Annersley was risking no extra noise from whistles, toy musical instruments or indoor fireworks! When everyone was decked in a crown, mitre, dunce's cap, bonnet or whatever else in the way of headgear came from the crackers and Blossom and two or three others had gone round with waste-paper baskets to collect the torn paper, they began on the speeches.

Elinor stood up and called, "Miss Annersley—Spee—eech!"

The school joined in, drumming thunderously on the empty tables with their fists and chanting, "Spee—eech—spee—eech!" until Miss Annersley rose to her feet. The noise ceased and they all turned to face her.

"What a *terrible* noise!" she said, laughing. "I should think they can hear you at the Sanatorium!"

The girls giggled appreciatively. Then they quietened down again and she went on:

"This is our first Spot Supper, but I know everyone hopes it won't be the last. Also, we are all very grateful to Miss Ferrars, whom you can thank later on, for giving us the idea. Now there are a large number of people to follow me, so I won't keep you any longer, except to wish you all very happy holidays and a return to school free from all infection and prepared to make next term a really record term!"

She sat down amid cheers and laughter which lasted until Julie Lucy jumped up, turned to her partner and shouted, "Miss Wilson—Spee—eech!"

Before she had got the last word out, the school had chimed in with more callings and thunderings and Miss Wilson bounded to her feet, protesting, "Oh, *no*! You're making more noise than ever. It isn't at the San they'll be hearing us, but right down into Interlaken and we shall have the gendarmerie along to ask what we're doing!"

Peals of laughter greeted this flight of imagination before she continued, "Well, we've come to the end of another term. I think it's been a good one, in spite of the weather. We have all the excitement of next term to look forward to—including," she added with a wicked twinkle in her eyes, "the public exams. What more could anyone ask?"

A small voice said in what was meant to be an undertone, but which came clearly across her dramatic pause, "No exams, of course!"

Miss Wilson herself led the laughter, while the people on either side of Margot Maynard hushed her in shocked tones. Joey, seated next to Julie Lucy, glanced down the room until she had singled out her third daughter and, having caught the young lady's eye, proceeded to mop her eyes vigorously.

Miss Wilson laughed again. "Well, I don't know about that. However, exams are on the programme, so you'll have to put up with it. That's all I have to say, except that I, too, welcome this innovation of ours, and hope it may become a regular habit."

185

Then she sat down and Kathie Ferrars was called on. She stood up, her cheeks flushed with embarrassment, though her eyes were dancing. Then some imp moved Blossom Willoughby to start. "For she's a jolly good fellow" in which the rest joined rapturously, and Miss Ferrars dropped back into her seat and hid her face in her hands.

"Oh, no, you don't!" Nancy Wilmot cried, leaning across Mary-Lou. "Up you get and give us your speech and no more nonsense! Heave her up, Mary-Lou and Katharine!"

Mary-Lou chuckled and looked at Katharine Gordon who was at St Mildred's this year, and expected to leave to go to London University at the end of the year.

"Come on, Katt! Up she goes!"

They tucked her hands under her arms and heaved her up and she stood between the two tall girls, crimson and laughing.

"It really is too bad!" she began. Then she stopped and the next moment she was beginning her speech which was a parody on *Hiawatha*.

> "In the pleasant Alpine mountains
> Where the sun beats hot in summer,
> Where the snows lie thick in winter,
> Stands that well-known school, the Chalet,
> Many-housed and many-pupilled,
> Staffed with many a learned lady,
> All prepared to work and labour
> For the good of all about them.
> Here I came, a shy young mistress,
> Here I ventured in the autumn
> When the tinted leaves are falling.
> When the sun in crimson glory—
> Crimson glory, flecked all golden,
> Sets too early in the evenings.
> Many friends I soon encountered—
> Friends of every age and spirit.
> Work and fun were all my portion

Meted out to me this portion
By the Heads who lead the Chalet.
Greatly have I relished all things.
Much have learn'd from all these new friends.
Now the second term is over
And I say with heartfelt warmness
May the school go on and prosper.
May its pupils also prosper,
Many golden laurels bringing
To its glory and its fair fame!
May it flourish fifty long years,
Aye, and more, a glorious century!"

Having delivered herself of this, she sat down amid
cheers and clappings. The girls had not expected *verse*—
even though it might be doggerel, and they were thrilled
with it.

But time was flying. Matron, with an eye on the clock,
murmured something to Joey and that young lady
bounced to her feet before anyone could call on her.

"You know," she said confidentially when silence fell,
"I do think it's most unfair to invite a person and demand
a speech from her! However, next term I'll be able to sit
smirking while other poor creatures stand as I stand here,
all hot and bothered."

Ecstatic titters greeted this statement before she could
go on.

"It's my only comfort," she said plaintively when at last
they were quiet. Then she grew more serious. "I do think
you girls are lucky to have a mistress who can hand on to
you a wonderful idea like this! I only wish we'd thought
of it when *I* was a pupil! But we never did. I'm glad to
see you appreciate Miss Ferrars. And I know that even
when she finally leaves us, whether to go on to another
school or to make a home of her own perhaps, she will
always be remembered in the school because she has given
us all this." A wide sweep of her hand knocked off her
partner's hat and provoked a squawk from that young
woman. "Sorry!" she said. "To go on with what I was

saying. Next term, we celebrate our coming of age as a school. We have had our ups and downs during those twenty-one years, but never, even during the months when we were in suspension, so to speak, has the school ever ceased *being* a school. We had to begin again with a small school, but, as you all know, we began to grow at once and we've gone on growing till now we have the Chalet School up here; the finishing branch, also up here; and Pelham House in South Wales—from which, I understand, we are to welcome some old friends and shining lights of former years next term. That's a pretty good record, I think. Girls! I want you all to go on doing your best to keep up that record. I've a right to speak because I'm the first pupil the school ever had. Further, though I may be a wife and the mother of nine, I'm still a Chalet School girl and I can't think of anything that would alter that." Loud and prolonged cheers greeted this and she had to pause. When the girls were quiet again, her gravity had passed and it was with a wicked twinkle that she concluded, "In fact, I expect to see my great grand-daughters come as pupils and to be able to quaver to them when they start rhapsodising to me about their school, 'Ah! But you should have been there in *my* time!' That's all, apart from my best wishes for happy holidays for every one of you, both staff and girls!"

She sat down amid a hurricane of cheering which lasted at least three minutes and only ceased when Miss Annersley, seeing nothing else for it, sounded her bell, keeping her finger on it until there really was silence and Julie Lucy, now Head of the finishing branch, could stand up and speak the few sentences she had ready.

After that, the other girls followed one after the other. Most of the speeches were very commonplace, the girls confining themselves to saying that they were glad they had come to the school and they hoped it would go on and prosper. Until it came to Charmian Spence's turn.

Charmian was an imp of the first order and after hearing what her form mistress and Joey had to say, she hurriedly scrapped her earlier remarks, and spoke extempore.

"I didn't want to come here at all," she confided to the startled school. "In fact I made a lot of scenes about it. I always thought England was good enough for me. But you know what fathers and mothers are like. No one would listen to me. So I came. And I did hate it when I found I had to learn to speak French and German. But I'm bound to say it hasn't been so bad as I feared. In fact," she wound up with one eye on Miss Annersley, "I might say I really am enjoying life here. And I hope that, like Mrs Maynard, *my* great grand-daughters will come to the school and I'll tell them all about what to expect before they do come, so that they won't make all the fuss that *I* did!"

She sat down in a stunned silence which was ended rather flatly by Elinor calling on Iris Woodley whose few words were very dull after Charmian's observations.

The last of the juniors finally got out what she had to say and then the girls stood up, pushed in their chairs and grace was said, after which they marched off to Hall where they settled down to an hour of sing-song. *Fhairshon*, *Willow the King*, *Forty Years On*, *John Peel*, *Silent, Oh Moyle* and many other favourites all had their turn. Then Joey was called on for a solo and gave them *Brittany* by Ernest Farrar, a young and coming composer who had been killed during the First World War. She was encored of course. Joey had been for many years the school's prima donna and now, with the years, her voice had grown and ripened till its golden sweetness had an added richness and maturity that made even the most unmusical junior sit still and listen with all her ears. She gave them the old Northumbrian folksong, *Blow the Wind Southerly* and then the lovely Scots song, *Caller Herrin'*. After that, she declined to sing solo again, but she did consent to be "Chanty Man" and led them in the Chanties, *What shall we do with the Drunken Sailor*? and *Rio Grande*.

"One last song," Miss Annersley said at last. "It's after nine and most of you people have the long journey tomorrow. What shall it be?"

At least a dozen songs were proposed—mostly by shouting—and were finally rejected in favour of the old negro ballad, *One More Ribber to Cross*. The girls let themselves go over it—and so did everyone else. The number of pairs that Noah had to take into his ark was amazing, for, not satisfied with the usual verses, girls in earlier days had added to the number, until, as Joey remarked aside to Miss Derwent who was sitting next to her, it must have been a fearful scrum in the ark!

"And now, that really is the last," Miss Annersley said firmly when it was ended. "What did you say, Joey?"

"Let's finish up with 'The day is past and over'. The girls will never go to sleep if they go up in their present hilarious mood. Dorothy!" she turned to call to Miss Lawrence at the piano. " 'The day is past and over'. You all know it, don't you?"

Yes; they all did. It was a favourite evening hymn with both Catholics and Protestants. Miss Lawrence struck up and young voices sang it very sweetly, led by Joey. By the time the last verse had been sung, they were all sobered down a little. Miss Wilson promptly took charge.

"St Mildred's! Go and get ready! And remember! When you get back, it's straight up to bed with the last one of you!" She waited until the last St Mildred's girl had left Hall, Miss Annersley standing at the doors to say good-bye to each of them.

Miss Wilson then nodded to Miss Lawrence before saying, "School—attention! Into line! Don't push, Emerence! Charmian, get level behind the next girl! Yseult—*Yseult*! You're out of line! Really girls! Do you want me to give you 'Files Cover!' I wonder? *That's* better! Thank you, Miss Lawrence! Forward—*march*!"

The school marched smartly out of Hall and upstairs, most of them going straight to the dormitories, for now that it was all over, some of them were yawning and sleepy and the rest were realising that they were tired and there was the long, all-day journey on the morrow. Only Elinor, with Sybil Russell, Blossom Willoughby, Hilary Bennet, Vi Lucy, who had been told earlier in the day that she was to take Amy's place as prefect next term and was jubilant, and Mary-Lou went to the prefects' room to finish the clearing up they had not done before supper.

"It's been a good term, hasn't it?" Blossom said as she dropped some scraps of paper into the waste-paper basket.

"Very good—and not too exciting," Mary-Lou agreed. She perched herself on the edge of the table and looked round the others. "You know, although the time is coming jolly quickly when our lot will have to say good-bye to the school, I do hope that when we're all as old as Auntie Joey is now we'll be able to say with her that we're still Chalet girls."

"Don't you worry," Hilary told her. "We'll say it all right! You get off that table before Matey comes along to see where we are and tells you tables aren't meant to sit on! And then help me tidy these books in here while the rest do a final picking-up and we'll get off. I know it doesn't matter about you. You're only going up to the Rösleinalp tomorrow——"

"That's where your toes turn in!" Mary-Lou cooed sweetly. She was well aware that she was going to give them all a shock. "I'm coming to England with all of you. Mother was on the 'phone to me just before supper and she says the doctors have given her leave to go home so we're all going—me first, to stay with Mr Howell and Gwensi and find someone to start cleaning Carn Beg and Mother and Dad are coming next week with Verity who's staying to help Mother pack. Won't it be fun to be at Howells again—though we shall miss Aunt Joey at Plas Gwyn horribly!" she added.

"Oh, well," said Blossom, who had recovered quickly from the shock, "it'll only be in the hols that you'll be there. You'll have her next door during the term and that's the best part of the year."

"Ye—es; but then I shan't have Mother and Dad up at the Rösleinalp. However, it's gorgeous news that Uncle Jack and the rest have given her a clean bill of health at long last. And anyhow, once I've got my degree, I don't suppose I'll be in England a lot," Mary-Lou said philo-sophically.

Sybil Russell had been thinking over their earlier remarks. "I don't know that I'd call this exactly a *quiet* term," she said. "If you ask me, we've had a fair amount of excitement. Arranging for the coming of age next term, and that young demon Charmian plunging us all into darkness during prep——"

"Not to speak of what happened at the panto," Vi put in. "That was excitement enough for anyone!"

"*And* the Spot Supper to wind up," Elinor finished the list.

"I didn't say it had been dull," Mary-Lou protested. "I only said it hadn't been too exciting."

"Quite exciting enough for anyone," remarked a new voice from the doorway where Matron had been standing unnoticed for the last two or three minutes. "And now, if you've finished, you people can be off to bed. Come along! Don't keep me standing here, waiting for you! I'm tired enough myself!"

Hilary shut and locked the cupboard door. The rest looked round carefully. Then they left the room and went off to their dormitories, Mary-Lou saying as they parted at the foot of the stairs to the upper regions. "Well, let's say it's been fairly calm. It has on the whole, even if we have had *some* excitements."

"I don't believe," Elinor said solemnly as she began to mount the stairs, "that this school will ever know what it is to have a term without excitements."

"*Are* you going?" Matron asked in exasperated tones. "If you don't, I'll march you all off to Miss Annersley for a good talking-to and that will be another excitement for you, though I doubt if you'll enjoy it!"

"Going!" Blossom cried, as she plunged past the Head Girl, nearly upsetting her, and went helter-skelter up the stairs. "But just you wait till next term, Matey! We'll all see some excitement for the Chalet School then!"

192